GHACHAR GHOCHAR

Vivek Shanbhag is the author of eight works of fiction and two plays, all of which have been published to wide acclaim in the South Indian language of Kannada. *Ghachar Ghochar* was excerpted in *Granta* and is the first of his books to appear in English. He is the recipient of  International Writing Program at

Srinath Perur is a writer and transl in *n+1*, *Granta* and the *Guardian*. I day *It Must Be Madurai*, published b, ...

Further praise for *Ghachar Ghochar*:

'One of the finest literary works you will ever encounter . . . Literary perfection is elusive, yet it is possible, as Vivek Shanbhag demonstrates in his magnificent novella, where comedy is undercut by seething menace and overwhelming regret at a failure to act decently.' Eileen Battersby, *Irish Times*

'This tragicomic novella is both a classic tale of wealth and moral ruin and a parable about capitalism and Indian society.' *New Yorker*

'A compact novel that crackles with tension, tracing the tangled path of a family's dissolution in their sudden rise to wealth.' *Kirkus Reviews*

'A story that packs a powerful punch . . . "What can I say – it is one of the strengths of families to pretend that they desire what is unavoidable." So perfectly put is this last line, it belongs up there with the now infamous opening of Anna Karenina, the clipped, exact prose of Perur's translation nevertheless ably conveying the rich depth of meaning therein . . . Shanbhag is the real deal, this gem of a novel resounding with chilling truths.' *Independent*

'Vivek Shanbhag is one of those writers whose voice takes your breath away at the first encounter. *Ghachar Ghochar* presents life and its undercurrents with limpid prose and quiet insight.' Yiyun Li, author of *A Thousand Years of Good Prayers*

'A remarkable novel about the fragile civilities of bourgeois life. The reader becomes absorbed in the unforgiving self-knowledge and expansive humanity contained in every page.' Amit Chaudhuri, author of *Freedom Song* and *Odysseus Abroad*

'Vivek Shanbhag is an Indian Chekhov, illuminating the romantic and financial tensions in middle class urban India with a doctor's precision and sensitivity.' Suketu Mehta, author of *Maximum City: Bombay Lost and Found*

'What's most impressive about *Ghachar Ghochar* is how much intricacy and turmoil gets distilled into its few pages. Vivek Shanbhag, who writes in the South Indian language Kannada and is translated here by Srinath Perur into clean, conversational English, is a master of inference and omission . . . There's a deeper loneliness in this wise and skillful book that no covering can conceal.' *Wall Street Journal*

'As always, fiction encapsulates a kind of truth with an immediacy and vividness that no amount of data and historical summaries can begin to approach. In just over a hundred pages [*Ghachar Ghochar*] distils the human soul's infinitely complicated relationship with money. Without Srinath Perur's precisely fluent and beautiful English translation, this jewel of a novel would have been little known even in India.' Neel Mukherjee, *Times Literary Supplement*

GHACHAR GHOCHAR

VIVEK SHANBHAG

Translated from the Kannada by
SRINATH PERUR

FABER & FABER

First published in the UK in 2017
by Faber & Faber Limited
Bloomsbury House, 74-77 Great Russell Street
London WC1B 3DA

This paperback edition first published in 2018

Published in the USA in 2017
by Penguin Books
An imprint of Penguin Random House LLC
375 Hudson Street
New York, New York 10014

Ghachar Ghochar first appeared in English
as an excerpt in *Granta* 130 (ed. Ian Jack)

Printed and bound by CPI Group (UK) Ltd, Croydon, CR0 4YY

A CIP record for this book is available from the British Library

ISBN 978-0-571-33608-1

2 4 6 8 10 9 7 5 3 1

In memory of Yashwant Chittal

GHACHAR
GHOCHAR

ONE

Vincent is a waiter at Coffee House. It's called just that—Coffee House. The name hasn't changed in a hundred years, even if the business has. You can still get a good cup of coffee here, but it's now a bar and restaurant. Not one of those low-lit bars with people crammed around tables, where you come to suspect that drinking may not be such a wholesome activity after all. No, this place is airy, spacious, high-ceilinged. Drinking here makes you feel cultured, sophisticated. The walls are paneled in wood to shoulder height. Old photographs hang on the sturdy square pillars in the center of the room, showing you just how beautiful this city was a century ago. The photographs evoke a gentler, more leisurely time, and somehow Coffee House still manages to belong to that world. For instance, you can visit at seven in the evening when it's busiest, order only a coffee and occupy a table for two hours, and no one will object. They seem to know that someone who simply sits there for so long must have a thousand wheels spinning in his head. And they know those spinning wheels will not let a person be. Eventually, he'll be overwhelmed, just like the serene spaces in those photographs that buyers devoured and turned into the cluttered mess we have around us today.

But let all that be—I don't mean to brood. Getting back to this Vincent: he's a dark, tall fellow, a little over middle age, but strong, without the hint of a belly. He wears a white uniform against which it's impossible not to notice an extravagant red cummerbund. On his head is a white turban, its tuft sticking out like Krishna's peacock feather. I can't help feeling when Vincent is around—serving coffee, pouring beer at a practiced angle, betraying the faintest of smiles as a patron affectedly applies knife and fork to a cutlet—that he can take us all in with a single glance. By now I suspect he knows the regulars at Coffee House better than they know themselves.

Once, I came here when I was terribly agitated, and found myself saying out loud as he placed a cup of coffee in front of me: "What should I do, Vincent?" I was mortified and about to apologize when he answered, thoughtfully: "Let it go, sir." I suppose it might have been a generic response, but something about his manner made me take his words seriously. It was soon after that interaction with Vincent that I abandoned Chitra and whatever there was between us. My life then took a turn that led to marriage. Now, let me not give the impression here that I believe in the supernatural—I don't. But then, neither do I go hunting for a rational basis for everything that happens.

Today, I've been sitting in Coffee House longer than ever before. I'm desperate for a sign of some sort. Part of me longs to speak to Vincent, but I'm holding back—what if his words hint at the one thing I don't want to hear? It's afternoon. There are few people around. Directly in my line of sight is a young woman in a blue T-shirt, scribbling something in a notebook. She's at a table that looks onto the street outside. Two books, a glass of water, and a coffee cup sit on the table in front of her. A lock of hair has drifted across her cheek as she writes. The girl is here at least three times a week at this hour. Sometimes a young man joins her for a coffee and then they leave together. It's the same table where Chitra and I used to meet.

Just as I begin to wonder if her friend will turn up today, I see him at the door. He takes the chair across from her. My gaze drifts away, then returns to their table with a jerk when I hear shouting. She's on her feet now, leaning across the table. One hand holds his collar. The other slaps him across the face. He's blurting explanations, forearms raised to fend her off. She releases his collar and throws one of her books at him, then the other, all the while screaming abuses that implicate all men. She pauses, eyes darting over the table in rage as if looking for something else to attack him with. He shoves his chair back and flees. She takes the glass of water in front of her and flings it at him. It misses and shatters against the wall.

She's surprisingly calm after he's gone. She picks up the books and her bag. For a few moments she sits with her eyes closed, breathing heavily. One of the boys sweeps up the broken glass. Coffee House had fallen silent as the few people present watched the scene unfold. Now the usual murmur resumes. On cue, as if this is all a play, Vincent goes to her table, and she raises her head to order something. It appears Vincent already knows her order and has it ready in the wings. A gin and tonic appears on the table suspiciously quickly.

I wave him over as he returns from her table. "What happened?"

Someone else in his place might say the couple is breaking up, or speculate that the man has been unfaithful. He might even observe that this is the first time the young woman has ordered a drink here. Not our Vincent. He bends down and says, "Sir—one story, many sides."

Had Vincent taken on a grand name and grown a long

shimmering beard, he'd have thousands of people falling at his feet. How different are the words of those exalted beings from his? Words, after all, are nothing by themselves. They burst into meaning only in the minds they've entered. If you think about it, even those held to be gods incarnate seldom speak of profound things. It's their day-to-day utterances that are imbued with sublime meanings. And who's to say the gods cannot take the form of a waiter when they choose to visit us?

The truth is I have no real reason to come to Coffee House. But who can admit to doing something for no reason in times like these, in a city as busy as this one? So I'll say: I come here for respite from domestic skirmishes. If all is peaceful at home I can think up other reasons. In any case, visiting Coffee House has become a daily ritual. My wife, Anita, to whom I once laid out the case for Vincent's divinity, sometimes wryly says, "Did you visit your temple today?"

Somehow, my unvoiced appeals seem to be heard when I'm in Coffee House. There are times when the thought of being there enters my mind just before going to bed, and I pass the night in a dazed half-sleep, eager for morning to arrive. I come here, pick a table from which I can see the goings-on on the road outside, and sit down. There are usually only a couple of people here at that time of the morning. Vincent brings me a strong coffee without my having to ask. I sit there and watch people pass by: in the cold of December they hurry past in sweaters and jackets; in summer they wear light, thin clothes, offering some skin to the sun. After gazing out of the window for half an hour or so, I call Vincent over, engage him in small talk, and root for pearls of wisdom in whatever he says. If the weather in my head is particularly bad, I might order a snack and prolong my conversation with Vincent. At times, I'm tempted to unburden myself to him. But then, what's the point when he seems to know without being told? These interludes at Coffee House, away from the strains of home and family, are the most comforting part of my day.

That girl who just chased her friend away reminds me of Chitra. I wonder how often Chitra must have thrashed me like that in her thoughts—I'd slipped away from her without saying a word. Her pride would never allow her to come after me, of course. Not once in all this time has she tried to make contact. I used to join her on most afternoons, usually at that very table. She worked for a women's welfare organization, and would gradually grow incensed as she told me about her day. The things she said about men I took as applying to myself. I could only sit there mute, feeling vaguely guilty. She might say, "How could you break her arm simply because the tea was not to your taste?" Or: "Do you kill your wife because she forgot to leave the key with the neighbor?" I knew that tea shouldn't lead to a broken arm, or a forgotten key to a murder. It wasn't about the tea or the key: the last strands of a relationship can snap from a single glance or a moment of silence. But how was I to explain this to her? There was no room for anything other than her anger. How, then, could there be tenderness between us? There was really nothing there, I suppose, certainly nothing physical. I never once held her hand, though I probably could have. When we had just gotten to know each other, I believed we might draw closer. But we never did. Then, one day, whatever there was between us vanished. I stopped going to Coffee House at our usual time and instead began going in the evenings. That was it—we never saw each other again.

I remember clearly what we spoke about the last time we met. She told me about a woman who had been turned out of her house in the middle of the night by her mother-in-law. While the woman shivered outside, her husband and his parents and sister all slept warm in their blankets. She'd sat there, hearing her husband's snores through the window. At dawn she hid her shame from the milkman by pretending she was waiting for the milk. Chitra's voice grew in shrillness as she described the woman's plight. "I'll make sure that husband and mother-in-law see the inside of a jail," she swore. "I must discuss the case with our lawyer before he leaves for home," she said and got up. She touched me lightly on the shoulder, said, "Bye, dear" as she always did, and left. It's all hazy now when I try to remember if I knew then that it was over. I do recall that I sat there quietly for a while after she left. I didn't show up at our usual time the next day. Or ever after. Chitra may have asked Vincent about me; I don't know. She probably realized I was avoiding her and never tried to get in touch.

As I sit here in Coffee House today, my mind is more disturbed than usual. If I can recognize it, so can Vincent. He knows I'm eager to talk to him, and he comes to my table of his own accord. I tell him: "Another lemon soda, please." He goes away after giving me a look that seems to say, "Is that really all?" In front of me, the girl finishes her gin and tonic with a couple of gulps and stuffs her books into her bag.

My mobile phone rings, startling me. Must be from home. It's been thirty hours since I left, and I'm worried about what news the call might bring. I look at the phone— an unknown number. I answer with some dread. It's someone asking if I want insurance. "No," I say curtly, and put the phone back in my pocket.

Vincent brings over a tray with a glass containing a mixture of lemon juice and salt, a bottle of soda, a tiny bowl with slices of lemon, and a long spoon. He places the tray's contents on the table with great deliberation. He produces an opener from somewhere in his cummerbund and pries open the bottle cap. As he pours, the foam comes gushing up in the glass. Vincent waits longer than necessary between pours of the soda, as if buying me time. I can pretend all I want, but how can I possibly hide from this all-knowing man the fact that I'm desperate to unburden myself?

TWO

Ours is a joint family. We live in the same house—my wife and I, my parents, my uncle, and Malati. Malati is my older sister, back home now after having left her husband. It is natural to wonder, I suppose, why the six of us should want to live together. What can I say—it is one of the strengths of families to pretend that they desire what is unavoidable.

The central figure in our household is my *chikkappa*, Venkatachala, my father's younger brother and the family's sole earner. He has a weakness for work, is at it night and day. We're in the spice trade—owners of a firm called Sona Masala. It's a simple enough business: order spices in bulk from Kerala, parcel them into small plastic packets in our warehouse, and sell these to grocers in the city. Chikkappa started the business, now our only source of income, and as a result he's regarded above everyone else in the house. His meals, his preferences, his conveniences, are of supreme importance to us all. The harder he toils, the better it is for us. He's unmarried, and we fuss over him so much that he's bound to wonder what additional comfort marriage could bring at his age. He receives all the domestic privileges accorded to the earning male of the family. At the first sound in the morning indicating he's awake, tea is made. When it's sensed that he's finished bathing, the *dosa* pan goes on the stove. He can fling his clothes in the bathroom or in a corner of his bedroom or anywhere at all in the house, and they'll materialize washed and ironed in his room.

Sometimes, on the pretext of work, he spends the night in his room at the warehouse. We're careful not to ask him about it. But a couple of weeks ago, there was a commotion when a woman came to the house. Chikkappa was at home, but he didn't step out. And why should he, when we're here to do battle on his behalf?

She came on a Sunday, at around nine in the morning. She'd waited awhile some distance away from the house, hoping perhaps to speak to Chikkappa if he emerged. It doesn't take long for someone standing aimlessly on the road to draw people's attention—my mother soon saw her from the kitchen window. She had on a pale green sari with a red border. Nothing in her bearing suggested she was a disreputable woman. Still, in the half hour or so the woman stood there, glancing from time to time at the house, my mother made several concerned trips to the window. In these matters, it is always the women who suspect first. The woman likely had no intention of creating a scene, and for all we know she might have been happy to leave after seeing Chikkappa briefly. But that was not what transpired.

She finally summoned the courage to approach the house. My mother saw her opening the gate and rushed out. By then she had made her way to the front steps.

"How can we help you?" Amma asked.

"Isn't this Mr. Venkatachala's house?" the woman asked, the hesitation evident in her voice.

"Yes. Who are you?"

"My name is Suhasini. Is he at home?"

"Whom do you wish to see?"

"I'd like to see him . . . Mr. Venkatachala. Can I speak to him?"

"Do you have some business with him?"

"I'd like to speak to him."

"Regarding?"

"Can I see him?"

Knowing Amma, she would have felt slighted by the

visitor's lack of forthrightness. But she held her tongue. After all, she had no idea who the woman was to Chikkappa, and it wouldn't do to displease him. "Wait, I'll call him," she said and came inside, leaving the woman at the door.

While this was happening, we, the three men of the house, were sitting at the dining table over our breakfasts, listening to the exchange at the door. Malati and Anita were in the kitchen, also within earshot. None of us acknowledged hearing anything.

Amma entered the room and turned toward Chikkappa. Before she could say a word, he began making signals to the effect that he wasn't home. This was all that Amma needed. She strode back outside.

"He's not home," we heard her say.

"But . . . he is."

"I said he's not home."

"Will you please mention my name to him?"

"How can I when he's not home?"

"He's here. I know he is."

"Am I lying to you, then?"

"I know he's inside. I saw him through the window. Please call him. I only want to speak to him."

"In which language must I tell you? No means no. That's all—now, please leave." It was clear from Amma's voice that she was nearing the end of her patience. I was amazed she could stand so firmly behind a lie.

"I will not leave without seeing him."

Malati went to the door to join the fray. Unable to resist my curiosity, I followed her and stood leaning against the doorframe. Up close the woman was attractive, slightly dark-complexioned. I could see a healed scar on her left temple and the odd grey hair amid the black. Her green sari had a fine brown pattern on it. In her hands was a small package wrapped in plastic. A black handbag hung on one shoulder.

Amma was emboldened by Malati's arrival. "Ey," she said, her voice now raised. "It's better you leave now. Do you want me to kick you out? Who do you think you are?"

The woman was taken aback by Amma's aggression. She seemed to realize the matter was getting out of hand. Making to leave, she brought out a steel container from the plastic bag in her hand and attempted to hand it to Amma. She said, "I've brought this because he's fond of it. It's *masoor dal* curry. Please give it to him."

"What is all this? Do you think we don't cook our own meals?" Amma was infuriated. She pushed the container back toward the woman.

"It's not like that . . . ," she said, and tried to press the container into Amma's hands. Amma shrank back and it fell to the ground. The lid shot off to one side; the contents formed a thick puddle on the ground. The smell of *garam masala* wafted into the house. We all knew that Chikkappa was fond of *masoor dal* curry. All of a sudden, the woman seemed crushed. She went down on her knees in front of the spilled curry, making helpless little noises. The liquid traced bright red trails along the ground, leaving behind dark clumps. The woman's affection for Chikkappa was evident. There was an awkward silence. I suppose we were all a little flustered now, and wondering what he would do.

The lull did not last. Amma burst into unprovoked invective. "Get out! Get out, you whore!" she screamed.

I walked back a few steps and glanced toward the dining room to see how Chikkappa was taking it. He had abandoned his breakfast and retreated to his room.

The woman had not abused us. She had not come here to pick a fight. We were thrown off balance by her love for one of us, and so we tore into her with such vengeance that she collapsed to the ground, sobbing. Amma and Malati called her a beggar, a whore, and it was clear from the disbelief on her face that she had never been spoken to in this manner. Perhaps she remained because she was certain that Chikkappa would come to her aid. That must have been Amma's worst fear, too, not that it stopped her.

On that day I became convinced that it is the words of women that wound other women most deeply. I'd never imagined Malati and Amma to be capable of such cruelty—they were like dogs protecting their territory. All that woman had wanted was to see Chikkappa once. But these two felled her with their words, and they kept at it as she sobbed, sitting there on the ground. Suddenly, she looked up through her tears as if searching the house behind us. She called out in a hoarse voice: "Venka . . . Venka . . . Come outside. It's me, your Tuvvi."

There was silence once more. She had deployed her most powerful weapon. It was embarrassingly clear now that there had been something between them. Venka and Tuvvi! Those private, affectionate names, now out in the open. Would he acknowledge this part of his life? We waited. If he was going to respond to her cry, it would be at once. Amma continued to stand firm, but I noticed her turn and glance into the house. When a few seconds passed without sound or movement from within, it became clear that Chikkappa wouldn't be coming out. A strange unexpressed fury radiated from the woman. Who knew how deep their relationship was? What mattered was that we had prevailed, and now all that remained was to bring the scene to an end.

Before any of us could say anything, she got up and left.

She walked briskly out of the yard and then turned for a moment to close the gate. Even now, when I recall the contempt in those eyes, it feels like someone just spit on me. She changed her mind about the gate, as if even the gate of such a house were too loathsome to touch. She walked off down the road and was soon out of sight.

There was no trace of Chikkappa. Why didn't he respond when she called him? He could have addressed her as Tuvvi, invited her in. He knew we wouldn't contest any decision he made. Then why didn't he? All that was left now was the smell of the curry she had brought, inviting enough to make one wonder if there might not be a little left unspilled in the container. Amma ordered that the container be thrown away.

Anita did not participate in the events of that morning. She'd remained inside the house, and she felt that an injustice had been done to the woman. But does being just necessarily entail shooting oneself in the foot? Even in the flush of their victory, Amma and Malati noticed Anita's dissent. It's an unwritten rule that all members come to the family's aid when it is threatened. Anita had broken that rule. She should not have.

Silence descended on the house. It was somehow rendered thicker by the lingering aroma of the woman's curry.

Amma must have sensed that this was the sort of silence that, left unchallenged, could consume the family from within. She began to speak nonstop. With no one else in the mood to talk, she fell upon our maid, Sarasa.

"Look, Sarasa, when you're buying a *dosa* pan it's not enough just to inspect the upper surface. You should look at the base, too. It, too, must have an even surface. And if you start using it from day one as if it's a nonstick—that's it! Your *dosas* will stick to the pan and come out a mess. There's a procedure to get it ready for use. In our house growing up we would apply oil to the pan and keep it near the stove's flame for several days. Sometimes we'd leave it out in the sun, too. After it was heated up we'd wash it, scrubbing it with coconut fibers. We'd keep doing this till the pan soaked up all the oil and became ready. An ideal pan should be coarse enough for the batter not to slide away, but smooth enough that the *dosa* shouldn't stick when lifted. That's when a pan is ready . . ."

She went on in this vein for a while. Sarasa emitted grunts of acknowledgment at intervals as she washed the pots and pans. Amma has a voice that fills the house no matter which room she's speaking from. On this day she raised it even higher. After a while she grew dissatisfied with Sarasa's responses and roped Malati in.

"Malati, ask Goyappa to come here for a bit if he visits the house opposite. Our jasmine creeper is wilting. I asked him to manure it, but he seems to have dug up the roots. Today is Sunday, isn't it? That's when he visits . . ."

"Which house, Amma? Meera's?"

"Yes, go tell Meera. She'll send him when he comes. The plant in your room's balcony also looks limp. Bound to happen if it isn't kept in the sun . . ."

No one noticed when Appa got up and went to his room.

I walked back to the table and, still standing, gobbled down the remaining piece of *dosa* on my plate. When I went to wash my hands, I noticed Anita glaring at me from the kitchen. Then she emerged, swept past me muttering under her breath, and rushed up the stairs to our room. I followed her, a little surprised.

"*I* didn't abuse her," I pointed out.

"It's enough for a man to simply stand there and watch. It's worse than shouting at her yourself. How could you all pounce on that woman without knowing a thing about her? Is it her fault alone? You should all be ashamed of your-selves. Not one of you had the guts to even hear her out. How could they treat another woman like that?"

I could not refute her. How was I to explain to her that Chikkappa must be protected at all costs? She wouldn't understand. For that, she would need to have lived through those earlier days with us—when the whole family stuck together, walking like a single body across the tightrope of our circumstances. Without that reality behind her, it's all a matter of empty principle.

THREE

Second in the family after Chikkappa is my father. He owns half of Sona Masala. Appa is a quiet man who lives in his own world, heading out somewhere like clockwork every morning and evening. If he dies without a will, his assets will be divided equally between me, my sister, and my mother. Our only fear now is that he might lose his mind with age and become ruinously entangled in some philanthropic enterprise. So we try to keep him in a good mood, making sure he doesn't lose his taste for food or develop other ascetic tendencies. We steer him clear of thoughts about the futility of life and so on. An unfortunate consequence of this is that we must endure his garrulity whenever he emerges from his shell—the same old stories, again and again. Who knows what pleasure he gains from reminding us of the days when we struggled to get by in this city on his tiny income.

Appa enjoys our current prosperity with considerable hesitation, as if it were undeserved. He's given to quoting a proverb that says wealth shouldn't strike suddenly like a visitation, but instead grow gradually like a tree. It's as if all we now have is nothing to him, and that is the root of our unease: What if this man loses his head, writes a will asking for his assets to be poured down the drain of some noble cause, and dies? Those swayed by lofty ideals don't think twice about doing such things. Casting one's own family out on the street is an achievement to them.

Appa used to be a salesman for a company dealing in tea leaves. His salary was barely enough for all of us to subsist in a city like Bangalore, but we managed to get by in a small, rented house. We had enough to feed and clothe ourselves; so what if the clothes were sometimes old. And if we didn't always feast, neither can it be said that Malati and I ever went to bed hungry. He also managed to look after Chikkappa like a son and put him through his commerce degree.

Appa's work began at nine in the morning and went on until eight in the evening. Every morning he would go to the company's warehouse, and set off in a small truck carrying packets of tea leaves. He'd go to the market areas due for a visit that day and refresh stock in local shops. The cash he collected was tucked away in a bag that hung from his shoulder and across his chest. He'd developed the habit of running his thumb and index finger along the strap like a priest stroking his sacred thread. He was inordinately proud of being a salesman. "What do you think a salesman is . . . ?" he'd boast, especially when launching into stories about his prowess—how, for instance, he'd managed to sell to a shop whose shelves were already brimming with tea. He polished his shoes every morning and put on an ironed shirt. He'd leave home looking like an officer and return at night, wilted from the day's sun, his clothes rumpled. One glance at his scuffed, dusty shoes was enough to betray the nature of his day's work.

After returning home, he'd have to finish the day's accounts. He would bathe, change into pajamas and an undershirt, have a cup of tea, and settle down to another round of work. On long sheets of paper the company provided, he'd enter the quantities of tea and coffee powder sold that day, the corresponding sums collected and outstanding. He'd sit on a mat in the middle room, surrounded by papers, his receipt book on one side, his money bag on the other. If the figures didn't match, he'd go over them again and again until they gave in and agreed. "Not one *paisa* should go astray" was his refrain while doing this. After he was done with the forms, he'd bundle the day's cash collection, tie it with a piece of thread, and keep it under the altar. The next morning he'd go to the bank, draw a demand draft for the amount, and send it to the company by registered post. With that ended the cycle of a day's work.

Appa's work was the whole family's work. We all knew the brand names of the various tea packets he sold, even the company's code numbers for them. Some days, Malati and I would help him with the accounts. The long leaf of paper was called a stock sheet. Malati would hold a corner so the carbon paper beneath wouldn't shift and I would race through the list of numbers. On a couple of occasions I discovered mistakes in Appa's tallies. Sometimes he'd talk to Amma about the people in his company. The most frequently recurring character was his boss, the sales manager—or "SM," as he always referred to him. We all read the letters and circulars that came from the company. They ended with "Happy Sales!" and I recall wondering what that could possibly mean, how something as demanding as sales could ever be happy.

Every year, he would take off for a day or two to another city for a sales conference, and return with a gift from the company. Our house's alarm clock, iron, and suitcase all came this way. As the conference approached, he'd recount to Amma the speculation in the company about that year's gift. We once went nearly a year without replacing our pressure cooker because of an unfounded rumor about what would be given at the conference.

Appa's salary seemed never to increase except for the odd year when sales happened to be good and he brought home a slightly higher commission. He had commitments to meet—he had to run the house, pay for our education and Chikkappa's. As a result of these expenses, Amma never got any jewelry from him. She brought it up on occasion, but she knew that it simply wasn't possible on our income. As long as the house ran on Appa's earnings his finances were known to us all. If we wanted new clothes, we knew exactly how much he could spare and what cuts would have to be made elsewhere. The result was that we simply did not desire what we couldn't afford. When you have no choice, you have no discontent, either.

One evening, Appa did his accounts and found a discrepancy of eight hundred rupees. This had happened before, so none of us took much notice. Appa drank another cup of tea and tried again. But the numbers wouldn't tally no matter how many times he redid the calculations. By ten at night, we were all worried. He refused to come to dinner until he'd found the source of the error. "Serve the kids. I'll come in a while," he told Amma. Malati and I sat down to dinner; Chikkappa joined us. Usually Chikkappa didn't involve himself in Appa's work, but that day was different. He sat down with Appa as soon as he had finished eating, and they began to go over the numbers together. Appa would look at his receipts and read: "Three eight zero. Eight zero five. One fifty. Sixteen. Two twenty . . . ," and Chikkappa would go, "Hmm. Hmm," as he ticked off the numbers on the sheet.

The entire day's account was redone, the cash counted again. The discrepancy remained. Amma called Appa in for dinner. He went muttering into the kitchen. The power went out as he was eating. Amma lit two kerosene lamps. She placed one in front of Appa and the other in the living room for Chikkappa, who was still trying to trace the missing money.

In the kitchen, a thread of dark smoke rose from the lamp. Amma questioned Appa as he ate: "Where did you go today? Did someone who was supposed to pay not do so? Did you count the money properly? Could you have put some of the cash in a different compartment of your bag?" Appa was angered by the interrogation. He finished dinner in a hurry, went out into the living room, and shook his bag empty. The lights came back on with a sudden glare.

"I have never placed cash anywhere else. That's our Ramana-sir's training. He'd say, 'Cash should never be in your hand except while counting it. It should either be in the shop owner's hands or in your bag.' Everything was in this compartment. Impossible for it to go anywhere . . ." Eight hundred rupees was an enormous sum for us. If it didn't turn up, Appa would have to make up the difference himself. Worse, the SM was due to visit in two days' time. "If this isn't sorted out by then, I'm finished," Appa said.

Malati and I slept in the middle room, which was also where Appa did his accounts each night. Malati fell asleep quickly. I lay awake and watched Appa, still frantic with worry, going through the receipts and cash yet again. I must do something to help him, I thought, just as sleep drew me away.

I woke up a little before dawn. Appa and Chikkappa were still there amid strewn papers. I heard the sound of pots and pans from the kitchen. My feet had extended beyond my blanket and grown cold. I drew them in, searching for a warm spot. Who knew when Appa and Chikkappa had woken up, or if they had slept at all. They were hunched close together and whispering so they wouldn't wake us up. Suddenly Appa exclaimed, "That's it! You're right. I think that's it. Pull out yesterday's sheet . . ." Chikkappa drew a long sheet of paper from a bundle, and they began to whisper again. Appa, who had been leaning over the sheet, relaxed and sat with his back resting against the wall. Chikkappa, too, looked up. There was a relieved smile on both their faces.

"This is it. We've got it. Twenty times forty," said Chik-kappa.

"The sixty-four somehow appeared as eighty-four. I looked it over yesterday but missed it. You've caught it now," said Appa, beaming at his brother. I had never seen them like that—sitting so near each other, talking. Their relief must have radiated into the kitchen. Before long Amma joined them. A moment I can never forget: Appa leaning against the wall, clapping Chikkappa on the thigh and looking up to tell Amma, "He spotted it." It was fleeting, but at no other point in my life have I felt so completely secure. "I'll make another round of tea," Amma said with visible excitement, and hurried into the kitchen. I sat up. I nudged Malati, who was sleeping on a mattress laid out perpendicular to mine. She was usually impossible to wake up in the morning—it took repeated attempts. On this day, however, she got up at once when I told her the news. There was a festive air in the house that made it feel like the morning of Deepavali.

Breakfast was *akki-rotti*. It's a special dish in our house, made only rarely. And I can't recall another occasion when Amma had been as generous with the chutney. There was an ebullience to her moving about the house, to how she patted the *rottis*, even to the way she sat on the floor in front of the stove. It felt like we had all come together and averted a calamity. The four of us sat in the kitchen in a row on the floor, our plates in front of us, chatting, in no hurry as Amma made the hot *rottis* one by one. As each *rotti* came, we'd tear it in four and quickly eat a piece each. By the time we were finished with breakfast, we had eaten much more than usual.

Appa reminded us that the SM was visiting in two days and proceeded to imitate his way of speaking. The SM was in the habit of punctuating his speech with the phrase "an important matter," but in his enunciation it became "unimportant matter." Amma usually grew annoyed when Appa was being silly, and she'd say, "Enough now. Stop it." Perhaps that was why the rest of us seldom responded to his jokes. On this day though, she joined in as we all laughed at the SM. Malati couldn't bring herself to stop—she'd stifle her laughter, raise a piece of *rotti* to her lips, and start laughing again. She even had to spit a morsel into her hand because she was unable to close her mouth. "First eat, then laugh," Amma scolded her, smiling all the while. I, too, joined Malati, laughing uncontrollably in solidarity. There was a closeness beyond reason in our kitchen that morning.

This time the SM turned out to be visiting on what was truly an important matter. He did not bring good news for Appa. Changes were being made to the company's operations. The distribution system was being overhauled and as a consequence all the salesmen were being pressed to accept early retirement. The SM had come down personally to break the news to Appa. Those were not times when you could change jobs easily. Losing one's job was seen as a disaster. By then Chikkappa had started working in a private company, but his salary was modest. The family was thrown off balance.

Appa had gotten ready and left early that morning despite knowing that the SM wasn't expected until the afternoon. "There will be a market visit. I'll be late returning," he repeated a couple of times before he left. "I've been seeing him all these years. A visit from him only means our targets for the year have been raised," he said more than once. Perhaps he suspected what lay ahead.

He returned unusually early. I was doing my homework in the middle room. It must only have been five-thirty or so. He entered and called out to Amma, who was in the kitchen with Malati. This was unusual, too. He stood with his bag still dangling from one shoulder, arm against the doorframe, and took off his shoes, one after the other. He came in wearing his socks, looked at me, dropped his bag listlessly on a chair, and went into the kitchen. A moment later I heard Amma's panicked voice say, "Oh my god!" I strained my ears but could not hear much. Malati soon emerged and told me what had happened: "Appa's job is gone. Seems he'll retire in two months. The SM was here to let him know."

Malati and I knew this was bad news, but its full implications were beyond us. I wondered if the SM had prefaced his delivery of the news with "unimportant matter," but kept the thought to myself. Appa had a cup of tea in the kitchen. Then he said, "I'll step out for a while," and left the house. I resumed my homework with a distracted mind. Malati was quiet. After a while she said angrily, "Who does that SM think he is?" and went into the kitchen, only to return at once. She beckoned to me. Amma was sitting in front of the altar, her hands joined. The room was lit only by an oil lamp. A strange fear took hold of me. I looked at Malati. She put a finger to her lips and led me out by the hand.

We didn't eat until Appa returned. "Come on, come on, let's eat," he said as soon as he entered the house, trying to pretend that everything was normal. Amma served us in silence. Appa went on and on. "Do you know how much they must have spent on the Deepavali decorations in the market?" he asked while the rest of us stared ahead blankly. He was not usually talkative at meals and Amma looked crestfallen to see him babbling like this. He noticed and tried to soothe her: "This just means I've retired a little early. I can work elsewhere after two months. There'll also be the retirement fund." He turned to me and inquired about school, something he never did. "When are the midyear exams?" he asked. I knew he was only making small talk, but I replied. I even volunteered information about the sports day. After all, we had to make the time pass somehow until Chikkappa arrived.

We abandoned all pretense when we heard the gate. Malati ran to open the door. Chikkappa must have realized something was wrong from the strange silence that greeted him. Tears welled up in Amma's eyes. Appa broke the news in as few words as possible.

As if releasing all the pent-up anguish of the last few hours, Amma broke down. "He still had eight years . . . ," she sobbed.

"Don't you start now," Appa warned, but her weeping went up a level. Finally he changed tack. "Look here," he said. "He hasn't eaten yet. Are you going to just sit there bawling? Heat up the food and serve him." He set her to work, which calmed her somewhat.

Amma lit the kerosene stove, not the gas. She had already begun to economize. "Don't ask me to use the gas from tomorrow," she said. "The sky won't fall if you wait ten minutes for tea." Appa told her he still had two months to go. "That will give us time to get used to it," she said.

When Malati and I finished dinner, we didn't leave the kitchen as we normally would; we sat there on the doorstep, side by side. Appa ate slowly, taking breaks in between morsels to tell Chikkappa details he hadn't mentioned to us.

"This is not about me alone. Our whole distribution system is being outsourced. There won't be any more salesmen in the company. They'll all be asked to retire early."

Chikkappa interrupted Appa's description of the new distribution system. "What do the union people say?" he asked.

"Oh, they've been silent for a long time now. Their mouths have been stuffed with cash. There's no other way now. Just take the early retirement, get whatever money is being offered, and leave the company. We'll see what happens. I can always look for a job afterwards."

"It's the same story everywhere," Chikkappa said. "Every company now prefers to work through these big distribution agencies. You might get a job with one of them. You have enough experience, after all . . . They pay better, too. A colleague's brother faced exactly this situation, and now he's earning more than before." The mood lightened somewhat.

Chikkappa splashed some buttermilk onto his plate, mixed in the remaining traces of vegetable and curry leaves with a finger, and drank straight from the plate. As he slowly picked up individual grains of rice still stuck to the plate and ate them, he brought up the matter of starting a new business.

"There's something I'd like to say," he said. "It's possible that whatever's happening is for the best. It might be time to make a decision." It all sounded very mysterious, but as Chikkappa spoke, it was evident from his tone that this was something he'd been thinking about. The rest of us sat there in shock. Our family had only known a salaried life. This was the first time anyone had thought of starting a business. Sona Masala was created that day in the kitchen. A crucial moment for the family, whose fate was about to take a sharp turn.

"This is the business my current company does. I've seen for two years how it is run. There's a fellow from Kerala who works with me named Kurup. He's said he will help in return for a commission. If it all goes to plan there's a lot of money to be made. The idea is to buy spices in bulk, package them, and sell them in the city. We can source the spices from Kerala initially, and then from wherever we get a good price. It's the sort of business where there's a good profit even when it runs only fairly well. And if the rates go up while we have inventory, we win the jackpot . . ." Though he was describing the business to Appa, he was speaking indirectly to the rest of us as well. We listened, spellbound. And perhaps with some fear, too. By the time Chikkappa finished speaking, the hand with which he had eaten had dried. Amma had forgotten about her own dinner.

Chikkappa may have had the business worked out, but he had no capital. "It's hard to get a bank loan unless you invest some of your own money," he said and went to wash his hands. Appa made his decision in the half minute it took Chikkappa to return. Appa told him: "My retirement benefits will amount to around one hundred thousand rupees. It's yours to invest. And then the banks will give you a loan. Start the business as soon as you can." That was all the encouragement Chikkappa needed. He had been in need of a spark to light the fire, and here he'd been handed a torch.

I've always felt that Appa's impulsive decision that day had something to do with all of us being present there in the kitchen. Who knows if he'd have come to the same conclusion if left alone to mull it over.

Then Chikkappa said to Appa, "You will be a fifty percent partner in the business." He's been as good as his word. Today my father owns half of Sona Masala's considerable assets.

FOUR

Amma, Malati, and I—we're tied for third place in the household hierarchy, though perhaps Amma occupies a marginally higher position since her entire life revolves around the house and family. She will go to any lengths to protect them—like that time she waged a war against ants.

The house we lived in when Chikkappa and Appa decided to start Sona Masala was in one of those teeming lower-middle-class areas of Bangalore. Small houses, all packed together. You could open our front door and be on the road in exactly four steps. Appa had been living there since before he was married. Our house had four small rooms, one behind the other, like train compartments. You could see right through the house if you kept all the doors open. The first room was just big enough for the wooden bench it contained. This was where Chikkappa slept. He sometimes returned late, and on those nights we'd leave the door unbolted so he could let himself in. He could go to sleep in the front room without waking the rest of us. The space beneath the bench was where we left our slippers and Appa his pair of shoes before proceeding farther into the house. Here were also stowed my cricket bat and my sister's umbrella.

The next room was the middle room, where Malati and I slept, did our homework, had our fights, and also where Appa did his accounts. It was the center of our domestic life, and I suppose was the closest thing we had to a living room. The next room received almost no light. It had a *pooja* altar in one corner and was used as a storeroom for grain and groceries. All our mattresses were stacked up there during the day, and Appa and Amma slept here at night. The room was a little damp, and the air made it feel different from the rest of the house. When the oil lamp in front of the altar went out, it would release a strand of dark smoke that filled the room with a sweet sooty smell. I often put off pouring oil into the lamp so this would happen.

Then came the kitchen, which was a little longer than the other rooms. It led to the bathroom, whose back door opened onto the tiniest of yards and a toilet. To go at night meant walking through the whole house. No matter how careful one was, the creaking of all those doors was hard to subdue. When it grew loud enough to wake everyone at night, Amma knew she had to oil the hinges.

The house had windows on both sides, but those on the right side looked over a drain and so were almost never opened. The windows on the other side allowed the smell of our neighbors' cooking to invade the house. They seemed to use great quantities of garlic, and the smell often overwhelmed us, disgusting Amma in particular. But during the day these windows had to be kept open so we could have some light. As soon as it was dusk, Amma would rush through the house, shutting them. There was hardly any furniture; the size of our rooms accommodated very little: a cupboard and a table for the gas stove in the kitchen; two green foldable metal chairs in the living room; a bench in the front room. There was no question of fitting any beds into that house; everything was done on mats laid out on the floor.

My morning alarm was the sound of Amma sweeping. At dawn she'd splash some water on the thin strip of stone between our front door and the road, scrape it clean with a coconut broom, and draw a small *rangoli* with rice flour. If it was cold I'd sleep a little longer, then wake up to the smell of breakfast spreading through the house. After Malati and I left for school and Appa for the office, Amma would wash the pots and pans, sweep and mop the house, and do the laundry. When Malati was old enough, Amma began trying to enlist her help with housework. But Malati had the ability to predict when she might be called on to do some work, and would vanish on one pretext or the other: homework, a bath, a school test, a friend's house, if nothing else an urgent trip to the toilet. This slipperiness was a source of some friction between her and Amma.

When he first started working, Chikkappa saved for months from his small income before managing to bring cooking gas to our kitchen. Along with it came the table the stove would rest on. There was such a bustle of excitement and anticipation the day the gas arrived. The workmen who brought the cylinder and stove placed them in the middle of the kitchen, put them together, showed us the flame, and left. We had already decided where to install the stove, but we went over the matter again at some length just to prolong the moment. Amma repeated at least ten times that she'd heard tea could be made in five minutes on a gas stove. She wondered if food cooked standing up would be as tasty. She joked: "Don't ask me for tea again and again simply because it will be quick to make." We had a long discussion about how the gas cylinder ought to be turned on and off to ensure maximum safety. Appa warned Amma: "Watch carefully now. You'll forget everything otherwise." And she listened quietly without putting up a fight. Amma had surveyed the neighborhood about its gas usage patterns. She told us how long a cylinder lasted in each neighbor's house and how it could be stretched. "If it's used only for urgent cooking, it lasts two months," she said. "Even when it's run out, it seems you can turn the cylinder upside down and get a little more." The inaugural preparation was to be a round of tea. I was sent out to buy some snacks for accompaniment.

None of us remembers when exactly the ant menace started. In the beginning, we'd spot an ant here and there, but after a while they took over the house. There was nothing we could do without knowing where they came from, and this was impossible because they were everywhere. Amma, who had to spend the whole day with them, would say, "They're not ants. They're evil spirits come here in disguise."

We had two types of ants. One was a small, brisk-moving black variety that appeared only occasionally. But when it did, it came in an army numbering thousands. These ants entered the house in orderly columns, then began to wander everywhere in apparent confusion, always bumping heads and pausing before seeming to realize something and rushing off in random directions. They had no discernible purpose in life other than trying our patience. It didn't seem like they were there to find food. Nor did they make the effort to bite anyone. Left to their own devices, they'd quickly haul in particles of mud and build nests here and there in the house. You could try scuttling them with a broom, but they would go into a mad frenzy and climb up the broom and onto your arm. Before you knew it, they'd be all over you, even under your clothes. For days on end there would be a terrific invasion, and then one day you'd wake up to find them gone. There was no telling why they came, where they went. I sometimes saw them racing in lines along the windowsill in the front room, where there was nothing to eat. Perhaps they were on a mission of some sort, only passing through our house in their self-important columns. But not once did I see the tail of a column, an ant that had no other ants behind it.

The other type of ant was a brown variety with more intelligence. They weren't particularly fast, but they had about them a clarity, a sense of purpose. You never found them rushing about aimlessly, killing time. But if there was as much as a speck of food to be had, they would somehow find out, turn up in orderly lines, and with great concentration haul bits of food out through a corner of the window or into a hole in the floor we'd never noticed before. These ants could drive Amma mad. She could not stand the feeling that everything we were eating had first been tasted by ants. She took to creating a moat around the food she had cooked, placing the containers in a pan filled with water. Even then some of the ants would try to swim across and perish in the process.

Any carelessness on our part—a box with a lid that wasn't shut tight, a serving spoon lying unwashed—immediately came to the attention of these ants. If a single grain of rice dropped outside a plate, you would see ants deliberating its transportation before you rose from your meal. If one of us brought a snack out to the middle room, ants would carry away crumbs we hadn't even realized we'd dropped. They'd gather around rings left by teacups on the floor. A mortar used to make chutney and washed a little too casually? Ants. Coconut grated and shell left lying around for a minute? Ants to finish off any remaining specks. Charred flakes around the edge of the *dosa* pan? Within no time—ants.

Amma was obsessive about washing the pots and pans. She'd scrub them clean immediately after she finished cooking. Malati and I were trained to wash our cups and plates as soon as we were done with them. Looking back, it's possible all this had nothing to do with cleanliness and was simply part of Amma's struggle against the ants.

But it was a losing battle. For all that we did to keep them at bay, they'd seize on the smallest lapse and invade. Just when we thought we had the upper hand they'd turn up in the most unlikely places. I once opened my pencil case to find it swarming with ants.

Amma resorted to chemical warfare—all sorts of powders and poisons. She made a dough from flour and Gammexane powder and sealed cavities behind which the ants were suspected of having their hideouts. Whether this killed any ants or not, it at least prevented Amma from feeling entirely powerless. The rest of us, too, were hardened by strife. It became a reflex to reach out and squash a stray passing ant. We'd flatten them with our hands or feet or books wherever we saw them.

On someone's advice Amma started treating the house with *neem* smoke. An old tin box was reserved for the purpose. About once a week, burning coals would be tipped into it over a base of sand, and handfuls of *neem* leaves thrown in. It produced thick smoke. Amma covered her nose and mouth with the end of her sari and walked the fuming box around the house, letting it linger in corners and behind the cupboard. Once I woke up in the middle of the night to go to the toilet and found Amma in the kitchen on her haunches, facing the wall, tracing the path of a line of ants with a flashlight. Now, unlike rats and cats, ants don't make things fall in the night and wake people up. I can only imagine the clamor they must have created in her mind. At one point, she even went around meeting officials and got the city corporation to fumigate the neighborhood. It's impossible to say whether it made a difference. We still had ants.

We had no compunction toward our enemies and took to increasingly desperate and violent means of dealing with them. If we noticed they'd laid siege to a snack, we might trap them in a circle drawn with water and take away whatever they were eating, then watch them scurry about in confusion before wiping them off the floor with a wet cloth. I took pleasure in seeing them shrivel into black points when burning coals were rolled over them. When they attacked an unwashed pan or cup they'd soon be mercilessly drowned. I suppose initially each of us did these things only when we were alone, but in time, we began to be openly cruel. We came around to Amma's view of them as demons come to swallow our home and became a family that took pleasure in their destruction. We might have changed houses since, but habits are harder to change.

The first time I saw our old house well-lit was the day we moved out. It's a day I will never forget.

All the windows on both sides were opened, and light came streaming into the house. Chikkappa had arranged for gunnysacks and cardboard boxes in which to pack our belongings. There wasn't that much to pack, so it only took about an hour. We loaded it all into a small Tempo. Appa left to accompany our things to our new home, sitting next to the driver. The house we'd lived in until then looked shockingly bare. Dust and the detritus of moving were everywhere. With their contents gone, the rooms looked even smaller and strangely lifeless. Where the floor had been covered by something, there was dirt along the edges. The wall behind the cupboard that held our pots and pans was caked with ant nests. Appa had argued against taking the old cupboard to the new house, but Amma insisted. For the first time, I wore my slippers inside the house. The crack in the wall of the middle room now seemed enormous. I'd had no idea our walls were so dirty. There were bits of paper lying about; dirt; dust on the tops of windows; a bright rectangle on the wall where we had hung the calendar; indentations where the backs of chairs had pressed into the wall; purposeless nails; a piece of paper soaked in oil; the smell of the kitchen. These scraps were the only remaining markers of our home. We were leaving something behind, though I couldn't say what. Amma must have felt something similar. For no good reason, she swept the house before we left.

Saying goodbye to the neighbors was a moment of both pride and worry. Our newfound prosperity was common knowledge in the neighborhood; still, our having bought a house, and in an upmarket area at that, was liable to provoke surprise and envy. So Amma did not dwell on the details. I suppose we, too, viewed our ascent with a touch of disbelief— could money acquired overnight also not depart with equal haste? As Amma and I went to each house, they all said, "Don't forget us. Keep visiting." At the age I was then, this seemed absurd. I had grown up among them—how would it be possible to forget these people? Now I see what they meant.

By the time we reached our new house, the Tempo had dropped off our belongings and left. Sacks and boxes were lying in the middle of the hall. The house was huge in comparison to the one we had left. Two stories. A room for each person. The smell of fresh paint still lingered. Our bench and two chairs couldn't make a dent in this expanse. Everything we'd brought from the old house appeared more worn, even unrecognizable in this new place. Soon, Chikkappa had a dining table with six chairs brought in. We'd visited the house twice before buying it, but it seemed different now that we'd moved in.

The kitchen had a counter on both sides, so all the cooking would have to be done standing up. There was no scope here for sitting on the floor. It was apparent at once that the old cupboard Amma had insisted on bringing along simply did not fit here. It was shunted to the backyard. There was no need for the gas-stove table, either, and this went to the storeroom. The bench on which Chikkappa used to sleep was installed on a balcony on the second floor. One chair each in Malati's room and mine. Everything we had from the old house was now scattered. Chikkappa brought home dinner. For the first time, we all ate together at a table.

"Feels like a hotel," Appa joked. No one laughed.

"We'll get used to it," Chikkappa said.

Chikkappa announced that he had set aside some money for buying furniture. He told Malati and Amma, "My friend owns a furniture shop. I'll take you there tomorrow. You don't have to worry about the price. Just pick out whatever you like. I'll pay for it all later." Never before had I seen Malati look so enthusiastic about a task assigned to her.

FIVE

Malati had always been unstable—a pile of gunpowder waiting to go off. All it took to light the fuse was our improved finances. She was in college when we moved to the new house. We'd been painstakingly frugal until then; what choice did we have? We consulted each other when money was to be spent, gave precise accounts. We thought of the family as being interdependent: a person who spent money was also taking it away from the others. All that changed overnight. There was enough now to buy things without asking for permission or informing anyone or even thinking about it. Appa's hold on the rest of us slipped. And to be honest, we lost hold of ourselves, too.

We needed things for the new house, and this freed us

in the matter of making purchases. For the first few weeks we bought as we had never bought before. Amma and Malati obeyed Chikkappa's instructions with diligence and emptied his friend's furniture shop. Soon the house was crammed with expensive mismatched furniture and out-of-place decorations. A TV arrived. Beds and dressing tables took up space in the rooms. In retrospect, many of the new objects had no place in our daily lives. Our relationship with the things we accumulated became casual; we began treating them carelessly.

Malati personified the chaos in our family. She'd always been quick to anger and inconsiderate of others, and those attributes found fuller expression in our new way of life. Her restlessness revealed itself in the harsh tone she took with others, and in violating the household's unwritten rules. She was the first in the family to start eating out whenever she felt like it. Then she'd pick at her food at home, which would lead to a tussle between her and Amma.

Until then, eating at a restaurant had been an infrequent treat. Every fortnight or so we would all go out for tiffin on a Sunday afternoon. Appa was in the habit of taking a nap after lunch on Sundays, and on the appointed day we'd wait impatiently for him to wake up, Malati growing increasingly desperate for her *masala dosa*. The budget was fixed—it bought a *masala dosa* for each of us and a single coffee shared between Appa and Amma. Sometimes one of us would ask for another snack. Then, Appa wouldn't feel like a coffee. You only had to see the plates off which Malati and I had eaten to know what we thought of the food—not a trace remained, even the chutney licked clean.

It wasn't easy to confront Malati. You'd have to listen to ten words for each one you spoke. Amma asked Malati once with some hesitation if she had eaten out. "Yes, Amma, I ate out," she said loudly. "I ate till I was full and then I drank coffee, too. What about it?" If anyone asked Malati where she'd been, she would give it back to them: "Do I ask you where you go? Why is it that everyone only asks me? Don't you trust me?" There was no one in the house who could stand up to Malati in a battle of words. Rather, there was no one until Anita joined the household.

It's true what they say—it's not we who control money, it's the money that controls us. When there's only a little, it behaves meekly; when it grows, it becomes brash and has its way with us. Money had swept us up and flung us in the midst of a whirlwind. We spent helplessly on Malati's wedding. No one asked us to; we simply didn't know how to stop. The main actors in that month-long orgy of lavishness were Amma and Malati. I don't think even they knew what they wanted. They'd set out every morning to shop, and when they were at home they spoke of nothing but saris and jewelry. The most expensive wedding hall we could find was booked. The caterer was dumbstruck by the number of dishes he was asked to serve. He would come to inquire about the menu and when he gave options of *chiroti*, *holige*, *jalebi*, *pheni* for the sweet, they'd say yes to all. He had only to mention a vegetable for them to say, "All right. Add that one, too." On the wedding day, after the ceremonies were over and the guests had been served, we all sat down to eat in the last round. Amma was weighed down in gold, beaming as she accepted compliments about the food. The couple was having their photo taken as they fed each other. Appa was sitting at the end of the table, looking dazedly at the plantain leaf crammed with food in front of him.

Perhaps it is not right to conflate Malati's short-lived marriage with the wedding expenses or our family's wealth. But I can't help wondering if she would have given up as easily if Appa had still been a salesman. Maybe she had gotten used to having whatever she wanted and it diminished her capacity for making the inevitable compromises that accompany marriage. Her husband, Vikram, was not a bad man. He ran the family business—a large sari shop—and worked from morning to dinnertime. He was free only on Sundays, but Malati expected him to spend more time with her. Initially they had small fights after which she'd come home in a huff. "He doesn't care," she'd say. "He would die for that shop of his." Perhaps her vision of an ideal life lacked room for hard work. Vikram, too, was helpless, having no source of income other than the shop. Her breaks from her husband's house began to grow longer and longer. In less than two years, she announced she wanted to leave him. Appa, Amma, and I went with her to Vikram's house to see if a reconciliation was possible.

We went on a Sunday afternoon around four. It had been cloudy all day. By then Malati had not lived there for three months. They received us in their large hall, where Vikram and his father engaged us in inconsequential talk. Malati was in the kitchen with her mother-in-law. I suppose we—all four men in the hall—were struggling to get to the point. We didn't have to. Just then there was a crashing noise from the kitchen. Malati stormed into the hall. Her mother-in-law, who was arthritic, limped out behind her, looking distraught. "Look what she has done," she said. "She's broken the whole tea set. It was such a good one." She was panting with rage and exertion.

"Tell them what you said first," said Malati, with a familiar curtness.

"What did I say wrong?" her mother-in-law asked. "I asked why she unpacked a new tea set, that's all."

"Why not a new tea set for my family? Why serve them in old, chipped cups?"

"We've never used old or chipped cups in this house.

There's nothing wrong with the cups we use every day. I only asked what need there was to open a new one, that's all . . ."

"And that's why I broke it. There's no need for it after all."

Her mother-in-law couldn't resist. "Is this what your parents have taught you?" she asked, in front of them.

"Yes. This is what they have taught me. You can ask them yourself since they're here. Go on, ask!"

It had all gotten out of hand. Vikram's father said to Appa and Amma, "Look, now you've seen for yourselves. How is it possible to get along when anything we say leads to a scene?" Malati's mother-in-law was in tears.

Vikram couldn't stay quiet any longer. "Why are you weeping, Amma? Everyone's seen how she behaves. Let her go stay in her parents' house if she doesn't like it here." His tone was not particularly harsh, but there was an obvious touch of male authority in his words.

His father raised his voice now. "Look," he said, pointing to his wife. "I've lived with her all these years and not once have I made her cry. It's only after this girl has arrived that I've seen her in tears."

Malati could hardly be expected to stay quiet. "Yes, yes, it's all my fault. You're all very gentle people."

Her mother-in-law wiped off her tears and said, "You can't buy graciousness. It's something that's handed down through the generations. They say the newly rich carry umbrellas to keep moonlight at bay . . ."

Amma was wounded by this. "Yes, it's true we've lived in poverty. That doesn't mean our heads have spun around because some money came our way."

It was clear that all this was not going anywhere. We rose to leave. They didn't ask us to wait. Nor did they come to the door to send us off. Malati led the way, still fuming. I felt it was mostly her fault, but I wasn't going to say anything while she was in this frame of mind. Appa hadn't said a single word all through the afternoon's farce.

The next Sunday I went to see a film in the afternoon. When I got back home, everyone including Chikkappa was sitting in the hall. Something about the way they were gathered struck me as ominous.

Appa and Amma were on the sofa. Malati was sprawled in a chair. Chikkappa was in the chair opposite her. Malati was somewhat triumphantly ticking items off on a list of jewelry. I knew there had been some concerned talk of recovering her jewelry from her husband's house. It seemed to have been done while I was out. Chikkappa greeted me as soon as I entered: "Come, come, you were the only one missing."

Malati started from the beginning for my benefit. "I

went there at one in the afternoon," she said. "I knew they'd all be home between noon and two. Chikkappa's friends were waiting in the park nearby. Their leader is called Ravi. He'd told me, 'You just get there and give me a missed call, sister. We'll be there in no time.'

"I went there and rang the doorbell. My mother-in-law opened the door. She refused to let me enter. 'If you don't let me in, I'll scream and make sure all the neighbors know what you're doing,' I told her. She said, 'Go ahead. I'm tired of your antics.' I quickly called Ravi from my mobile. He and his friends were there in no time, six of them, hefty men. My mother-in-law was scared. 'Who are these people?' she asked me. 'Just my uncle's friends,' I told her. 'Are you trying to scare us?' she asked. Just then Ravi pushed her aside and entered the house. Vikram and his father emerged from within. 'What's all this? Who are these people?' Vikram shouted, looking at me. 'I'm going to call the police,' he said. And then you know what? Ravi simply stepped up to him and gave him a sharp slap. You should have been there! Vikram was so scared. 'Please, sir, don't hurt me. Please,' he started saying. I wanted to laugh. He was actually calling Ravi 'sir'! I told Vikram, 'Look here, I've just come to take my jewelry. I only want what belongs to me. You can keep whatever your parents gave me.' He didn't say anything. 'What? Did you hear what she said?' Ravi asked, taking out a long knife and placing it on the table. One of Ravi's guys shut and bolted the front door from inside. I went into the bedroom. The keys to the *almirah* were still where I remembered them. My gold was all in one box, lying there since the wedding. I brought it out with me. I took my *taali* and the bangles they had given me and threw them at my mother-in-law's feet. You should have seen their faces! Vikram's father was sitting mute in a chair. Ravi was speaking to Vikram in a low voice. Every time I heard Vikram calling him 'sir' I had to stifle my laughter. I opened the box in front of him before leaving. 'I've only taken what is mine. See for yourself,' I said. He didn't look. He didn't say a word. I left. Ravi called sometime before you got here. He said they sat there for a while after I left and even had my mother-in-law make tea for them. He's warned them that the matter better end here, peacefully."

Chikkappa was sitting in his chair, looking very pleased with what Malati was reporting. Amma didn't approve of the phone call. "Was it so important to report that they had tea?" she asked.

Appa didn't seem happy with the day's events. "This means we've broken all relations with them," he said to Malati. "You shouldn't have gone there and frightened them like that."

Chikkappa cut in: "They're all my friends, nothing to worry about. Don't family members go in these circumstances and bring back valuables? Same thing. It's also their work. They call themselves recovery agents. It's these times we live in . . . Nothing is straightforward. If I didn't use their help to get payments due to Sona Masala, all I'd be doing is walking from street to street, knocking on doors."

Appa got up and left the room. My guess is that Amma didn't approve of these rough methods, either, but she would never say that. "Where's today's paper?" Chikkappa asked, indicating there was nothing more to be said. Malati went to her room. I followed soon after. When I passed the closed door of her room I thought I heard sobs from inside. Perhaps it had all gone too far, and she was being pushed down a path she really didn't want to take. I wanted to go in and console her, but I didn't know what I would say. And what if she thought it a loss of face to be seen crying? I went on to my room.

Amma had hopes that Malati's marriage could be salvaged. I suspected that Malati was not entirely indifferent to Vikram either; perhaps she even loved him. But she settled in at home and attempted no reconciliation. Nor did he. None of us had the courage to ask her where she went or what she was up to. Occasionally, she halfheartedly helped Amma with the housework. But this was aimed only at asserting her position in the house, and it became more conspicuous once Anita joined the household. The rest of the time she was thumbing messages into her phone. Sometimes I heard her on the phone late at night and wondered who it could be. That Ravi? Or was it possible she was softening toward Vikram and meeting him without the knowledge of the families? Malati forever invoked a friend named Mythili with whom she would watch films, at whose place she would stay, in whose company she would take trips to Mysore and Madras. I suspected this Mythili was a front behind which she was having an affair with someone. But even if that were true, what could I have done?

Malati's restlessness, her lack of peace, touched all of us. She was outspoken, rude, aggressive, it's true; yet we had lived for years in some sort of harmony. How could that aspect of our life together have vanished entirely? In the middle room of the old house where she and I used to sleep, sometimes we'd chat late into the night and she would confide in me. She told me about her college, her classmate Vandana, whose stepmother served her leftovers, and who was in love with a boy they called Koli Ramesh. It was Malati who carried letters between them. In the new house, we were locked in the cells of individual rooms, and there was no opportunity to exchange casual confidences. Lying alone in my room, I sometimes wondered if Malati's happiness would have been better served had Sona Masala not existed at all.

It isn't easy for a woman to leave her husband and live in her mother's house. In our case, the trouble was not so much the people who lived there—we were ultimately on Malati's side after all—but others: guests who visited home, people we would run into at weddings, well-wishers ever eager to put us on the defensive, busybodies. We all grew a little paranoid, suspecting malice on the part of anyone who spoke to her. Terrible stories spread about her after she got back her gold from Vikram's house, stories in which she was made out to be an incarnation of Phoolan Devi: she had led a band of goons and ordered them to vandalize the house; she had herself held a knife to her husband's throat. I know she could have done without all the talk. I'm sure she, too, wanted to live a regular, happy life, but things had somehow gone awry. I'm not sure how. Perhaps it isn't right to place the entire blame on Sona Masala, I don't know.

SIX

Now, what can I say of myself that is only about me and not tied up with the others? Wherever I try to start, I quickly run into one of three women—Amma, Malati, or Anita—each more fearsome than the other. I sometimes wonder if their every moment is spent sharpening their tongues, silently accumulating resentments for later use. And then, when they're in the mood, they'll whip up a storm that gives me the shivers even to think about.

It might start when I finish my bath in the morning and call out casually, "What's for breakfast, Amma?"

Amma says: "I've made *avarekaalu upma* because you like it."

It seems an innocuous enough statement. An outsider

may not be able to see its explosive power. But as someone who lives in this house, I know just how grave the consequences can be. I start hurrying to leave the house before it erupts. I jump into my clothes, scramble for my bag. And right then Anita might say to me, just loud enough for the others to hear: "I hope the prince will eat in comfort. So what if the rest of us starve." The reason: she can't stand *avarekaalu*, to the point where she throws up every time she smells the beans. It's true I like them, but I don't need to have them. But ever since Amma learned that Anita despises *avarekaalu*, she buys them every time she spots them in the vegetable market. She can do this because she controls the kitchen. There's a daughter-in-law, there's a daughter who's left her husband and set up camp here, yet Amma clings to the kitchen. It's not her fault—it's all she knows. In any case, Anita doesn't like to cook. It's not that she can't; she doesn't want to. Then there's Malati, about whom Anita often says, "If she wasn't like this, the situation in our house would have been so much better." I wouldn't dare agree even in private, but I know in my heart that she's right.

Even if Anita's jibe about princes and so on is made to me, it is directed at Amma. Amma flares up every time Anita speaks disrespectfully to me, or makes barbed remarks about my sloth or my tendency to procrastinate or brings up the fact that my rightfully earned personal income is precisely zero. It's also Anita's often-repeated allegation that this last fact was not properly revealed to her before our marriage.

These three address each other indirectly—that is the prelude, the shot fired in the air to challenge an adversary to battle. The idea is to inquire if the enemy is prepared and willing to fight. If there's enthusiasm on the other side, a reply is heard. That, too, is aimed at no one in particular.

"Oh, since this house is crawling with cooks, each member of the family can be served a different dish," says Amma. How can Anita stay silent? She drags her sister-in-law into the ring: "The house has turned into a shelter. This is what happens when all sorts are taken in. People should live in their own houses . . ."

This, of course, is a reference to Malati. Malati might wait to see if Amma comes to her defense. If not, she's perfectly capable of holding her own: "Why just a shelter, it'll soon be a brothel. When the men in the house aren't firm, the women will stand at the windows."

This particular arrow from Malati is aimed jointly at Anita and me. It's a canard built on Anita being friends with a man in the neighborhood. They were at school together in her town and happened to meet again here. I'm certain there's nothing between them, of course. But it turns out that both Malati and Anita find it unbearable that

I'm not in the least a suspicious husband. Anyway, at this stage of the conflict, Anita can rope my father in as well. "Hmm. It takes some talent even to joke. Mindless babbling doesn't make anyone laugh. But then, these things are in one's blood perhaps . . ."

That might sound like a tame comeback, but the sword of insult seldom cuts on the surface. No, it lacerates from within and leaves wounds that reopen with remembrance. Anita's remark is a savage mockery of Appa. He attempts compulsively to say something funny all the time, and this has turned him into an object of laughter. No one is amused by his quips; making matters worse, he laughs at his own jokes. That laughter, too, has increasingly grown feeble and nervous and altogether pathetic. All this is perhaps not unrelated to the fact that a while ago, he grew so listless that he was prescribed a course of antidepressants. Anita's remark about jokes feels innocuous, but it carries with it painful associations. The rest of us become flustered and try to ensure Appa doesn't hear any of this. Anita sees victory in our flapping about. Doesn't she know our entire future is perched on a will Appa hasn't written? What can one say about such suicidal behavior?

After all this blowing of war bugles over the *upma*, I don't even eat it. I rush out and arrive at Coffee House just as it is opening. I sit down, order a vegetable cutlet and a coffee. I make some small talk with Vincent: "So, Vincent, what news?" He says, "Holes in *dosas* in everyone's house, sir." A common enough adage, it's true, but am I to believe he brought it up with no knowledge of the morning's events? In any case, I sit there with my coffee and brood over what might have happened after I left.

The day's routine at home is a matter of speculation to me. I leave in the morning for Coffee House, carry on with my day, and only return after dark. I stay out all day like any other office-goer, killing time with great dedication. I wasn't always like this. It started after I finished my degree and a position was created for me at Sona Masala. I even got an office to myself. Chikkappa had once told me while I was in college: "Come join us after your studies and help us grow the business. Don't go and work for just anyone." And I didn't work for just anyone. Nor did I work at Sona Masala. I didn't work at all.

How did I slip into this way of life? I can only look back and wonder. I recall a time when I received daily lectures about how I had to study well and find a job. The pressure eased when Sona Masala began doing well. The family no longer looked to me as the person who'd one day have to provide for us all. Instead, there developed an unspoken understanding that I'd end up helping Chikkappa with the business. I began going to the warehouse when the time came. But it was clear from my very first day that they had no real need for me. They'd assign me a few trivial tasks because I was there, but nothing of significance ever got done without Chikkappa's approval. Soon I was bored out of my wits. At times I'd come into a fit of enthusiasm and try to change something, but I didn't know enough about the business and would only end up burning my fingers. My attempts at actually working there lasted no longer than six months. I eased myself out, almost without realizing it.

But still, it is the duty of the family to preserve my self-respect. I would be married one day, and I shouldn't have to suffer the indignity of holding my hand out for money while my wife watched. So, a monthly deposit began to be made to my bank account. It goes on to this day. Who would work when they get paid for doing nothing? With the exception of Chikkappa, of course, who knows nothing other than work.

This is my typical routine: I finish my bath and, on peaceful days, eat breakfast; I get ready and leave home for Coffee House at the appointed time. From there I go to the warehouse, sit in my office, and read three newspapers from beginning to end. Lunch. A nap on my office sofa. Tea. As the sun goes down, I set off again for Coffee House. From there I saunter about for a bit and eventually drift homeward. No one at the warehouse has a reason to enter my office except whoever cleans it before I arrive in the morning. I don't step out, either. From time to time, I sign wherever Chikkappa jabs his finger, and that's all the work I do. My business cards are reprinted every year. They say I'm the director of the firm.

I didn't put up a fight when the family began efforts to get me married. None of my attempts at romance had gone anywhere. Chitra was the only one with whom I'd even gotten as far as having long conversations, and that was over. Because Malati's marriage had ended badly, Amma was more circumspect when it was my turn. "Let's not get entangled with rich people," she said, and so when we received word about the daughter of a college lecturer in Hyderabad, she was inclined to pursue the matter. The alliance was brought to us by a friend of the family named Sripati.

It was a Thursday, at about ten in the morning. I was about to leave home for the day when Sripati arrived. "Wait, wait, wait, don't go!" he said. "It's you I've come to talk to." He chatted with Amma about mutual acquaintances, reported on his visit to the Raghavendra Swamy temple, delivered gossip from the attached monastery, ate *dosas*, proceeded in stages to make himself comfortable, and finally broached the subject. "Look, this girl is good as gold. She's done her BA. The father is well respected. He has made his name in the university. We were actually looking at her for my sister-in-law's brother, but he never turned up from the United States. There's some talk he might have married there, but who knows . . . Anyway, if you all agree, I can put the matter to the girl's father. Of course, I can't guarantee they'll say yes. Times have changed, it's not like the old days . . ."

I looked at her photograph and found her prettier than the other girls I had seen. I decided to make her mine before other proposals came her way. It all went quickly from there.

When we came to the matter of seeing the girl, I corrected Sripati with what I had picked up from Chitra's feminist talk: "We should speak of the boy and the girl both seeing each other."

He said, "Yes, yes! Of course! I meant exactly that. Is it even possible these days to arrange a marriage with only the boy's consent? I must say you are well-matched. Her father, too, thinks along these lines."

A couple of days later, on Sunday, we booked a car and set off for Hyderabad. Sripati accompanied us. Anita and her parents met us at the hotel we were staying in, and it wasn't long before the match was agreed upon. I took Anita down to the restaurant for a coffee; that was the only time we had to ourselves. The wedding date was fixed before we left Hyderabad. It had all gone by like a dream.

On the journey back, Sripati told us at great length about Anita's father's idealistic views. This was probably meant to soothe Amma, who had taken offense at something he said. When Anita and I were away, having coffee, Amma had announced grandly that we didn't expect a dowry. It seems Anita's father said, "I wouldn't give my daughter to you if you asked for one." Amma, who'd been enjoying her own magnanimity, was not pleased. As we were returning to the room from the restaurant, Anita had told me she would visit Bangalore soon so we could meet again. But her father had a heart attack shortly thereafter, and she couldn't leave Hyderabad. We next met at our wedding. I did call her on the phone before that, though.

"When are you coming here?" I would ask, trying to sound flirtatious.

I wanted her to say, "Now," but received only a matter-of-fact "The day before the wedding."

I'd persist: "Come right now."

"Don't be silly," she'd say, dousing my ardor with cold water. I couldn't help wondering at times if she was truly enthusiastic about the marriage.

Our wedding day was a momentous one for me—a woman entered my life for the first time. Until then I had never even held a woman's hand. That day I discovered the exhilaration of getting married in the traditional way. What

I'm saying might be incomprehensible to couples who have spent time together before marriage and for whom the wedding comes as a formality. They'd probably just laugh and call mine a case of sour grapes. And maybe they're right—it's true that things didn't happen this way because I wanted them to. But a few details from the wedding day might help explain what I mean.

In the days leading up to the wedding I couldn't resist gazing at her photograph from time to time. That's when I would call her on the phone. I had two photographs of her, both brought by Sripati when he first proposed the match. One of them showed her standing in a pink sari. Somewhat curly hair. Thick eyebrows. Broad shoulders. She seemed to be glowering at the camera, but there was something hypnotic about those wide eyes. I found it hard to look away. She was in profile in the other photo, wearing a *salwar-kameez*, looking out a window. She held a window-bar with one hand. Her face glowed with light. This photo drove me wild. That slightly upturned nose, the swell of her breasts discernible through the fabric of her *dupatta*. I suppose Chitra was right when she said men were incapable of seeing beyond the bodies of women.

On our wedding day Anita looked more beautiful than I'd been able to imagine her. She carried herself with poise. Her thick braid hung down to her waist. She was wearing lipstick. The first chance I got, I stole a sideward glance at the blouse under her dark blue sari. We had few opportunities to speak during the wedding ceremony, which we used to say things like: "So much smoke"; "Who's that teasing you? A classmate?" There was a strange charm even in exchanging inanities. The ceremony required me to hold her hand at times, or touch her arm with my index finger, and these brief moments of contact caused an immense thrill. When it was time to tie the *taali* around her neck, I leaned in close and a whiff of fragrance went straight to my head. The scent of flowers and her close presence were almost too much. For a brief instant I felt unsteady on my feet. She stood there with her head bowed; flecks of turmeric dotted the down on her cheek. My fingers brushing the back of her neck, I tied the knot.

At lunch, when we had to feed each other sweets, the tips of my fingers touched her lower lip for a moment. The jolt this produced took a while to subside. I was still helpless when she brought a piece of *jalebi* to my mouth. I seized her hand and pretended to bite off her fingers. A few girls nearby went, "Aww, so sweet," and I felt embarrassed by my own antics. The wedding photographer, hankering for such moments, made me feed her again.

While we were still at lunch, a large group from Anita's side came up to us and introduced themselves one by one.

Then, in the afternoon, an army of elders from both sides took turns sitting on a chair so we could fall at their feet and seek blessings. In the evening we went home exhausted. Fortunately, the more annoying relatives didn't follow us home. We could have dinner in peace and retire to our room upstairs.

I had on a white cotton *kurta* bought specially for the night. My mind swirled with the possibilities that lay ahead as we made our way to the room. I found it hard to even look at her. I tried to act casual as I closed the door behind us, but slid the bolt in slowly so the others in the house wouldn't notice. When I turned around she was standing by the bed. The light switch was next to the door and I turned it off. The room was now faintly lit by the haze from the streetlamp outside. I walked up to her. I took a step closer. I could smell her scent now. I didn't know what to do next and I paused for a moment. Then I raised my right hand and placed it on her shoulder. One thing alone gave me the courage to touch her: we were married now. My hand lowered itself along her arm and stopped at her elbow. My left hand went to her waist and drew her closer. She moved toward me as well and we embraced. Her touch, her smell, the fragrance from the flowers she was wearing, the press of her chest on mine, her lips against my neck.

That single moment's intensity hasn't been matched in

my life before or since. A woman I didn't know had chosen to accept me, in body and mind. Perhaps it is this instant that forms the basis of traditional marriage—a complete stranger is suddenly mine. And then, I am hers, too; I must offer her my all. I want her to wield her power over me as an acknowledgment of my love. The rush of these feelings all at once is too much to describe. Language communicates in terms of what is already known; it chokes up when asked to deal with the entirely unprecedented.

Similar feelings must have welled up in her, too. Her face was buried in my chest. Her arms tightened around me. I could feel the bangles on her arms pressing into my back. Through touch, through the giving, yielding closeness of our embrace, this unknown woman began to be known to me. I've often longed for a comparable experience, but there seems to be none. That sense of strangeness, surrender, dependence, compassion, entitlement, and a hundred other sentiments bundled together cannot possibly be relived.

I held her tighter still, then relaxed. I raised her face and through her lips gained my first taste of her world.

Three days after the wedding, we left for Ooty for our honeymoon. A cliché, it is true, especially considering we were well-off and could have gone anywhere. But Anita said she didn't particularly care where we went, and Ooty had been a prominent setting for my amorous imaginings since I was an adolescent. We might as well go there, I thought.

We were to arrive early in the morning, but the bus broke down on the way and it was noon before we checked into the hotel we had booked, a place called Green Valley. With the door to our room closed, we were away from home and truly by ourselves for the first time in our marriage. Not knowing what to do, but aware this solitude was too significant to be wasted, I began caressing Anita haphazardly. She shied away, played coy, and we ended up laughing and chasing each other around the room like children.

We washed, had lunch, and took a van to one of those sightseeing points on top of a hill. Afternoon was turning to evening. The air was crisp and our breaths had begun to fog. As we strolled about, Anita occasionally took my hand in hers or I would hold her lightly around the waist. Before long I was aroused and wanted to take her back to the hotel. But there were four other couples sharing the van with us, and we had to wait for them. It was dark when we returned. The wait had driven me half mad. I closed the door and pounced on her. I tore off her sweater, her sari, her blouse. I yanked at the drawstring of her underskirt but only managed to jam it up. My impatient hands couldn't get anywhere with the stuck knot. She tried, too, but to no avail. "Tchah," she said, "this string has become all *ghachar ghochar*. Wait." I stood there as she sat up, bent over the knot, and carefully teased it apart.

It came back to me later when we were lying there catching our breaths. "What was that you called the under-skirt string?" I asked her.

She giggled. "*Ghachar ghochar*," she said.

I'd never heard the expression. "What's that?" I asked.

"*Ghachar ghochar*," she repeated, her eyes shining.

"What does that mean?"

"It means just that. You wouldn't understand . . . ," she said.

I poked her bare side with a finger and began to tickle her, saying, "Tell me now, tell me."

She rolled about, helpless with laughter, and then went quiet with mock gravity. She said, "There are only four people in this world who know what it means. My parents, my brother, and I."

The expression had originated in their house, made up by Anita and her brother when they were children. They were on the terrace one evening, rolling kite string into a ball. Their parents were chatting nearby. The loose string strewn about became so entangled that her brother lost his patience, flung down the bit he'd been trying to separate, and shouted, "This has all become *ghachar ghochar*!" Anita said, "What language are you speaking?" From there it had entered the family's vocabulary, first used by the siblings and then by the parents. Anita couldn't stop laughing at the reminiscence; I joined her. She spoke of her family some more. She became grave when she came to her brother, who had lost a leg in a motorcycle accident. "He fell in with the wrong people and everything became *ghachar ghochar*," she said. "Otherwise, he wouldn't have been roaring around on motorcycles."

The next morning, we woke up in a hopelessly rumpled bed. I entwined my legs in hers and said, "Look, we are *ghachar ghochar* now." She did not laugh. She must have thought I was making fun of her. Of course, those words could never mean to me all that they meant to her; nor would I ever utter them as naturally as she did. But she had shared with me this secret phrase that didn't exist in any language, and now I was one of only five people in the world who knew it.

The week we spent in Ooty was easily the best time of our life together. Still, there were occasions when we found ourselves at odds. One morning we had just woken up and were watching the sunrise from the window as we sipped tea. I noticed an ant on the window frame and casually jabbed at it with my forefinger. I turned when I noticed she was looking at me.

"Why did you do that?" she asked.

I looked at her, uncomprehending.

"What had that poor ant done to you? Why did you kill it?" she asked, her eyes filling up with tears.

How was I to explain to her my history with ants? It would make no sense to someone who hadn't lived through something similar. "I'm sorry," I said, trying to close the matter quickly, and in return received a lecture about the senseless violence human beings indulged in.

Anita was also upset when she asked about Malati's husband and I told her what had happened. I didn't wish to hide anything from her. But her horrified expressions sometimes kept me from telling her everything. Those days in Ooty made me certain of one thing: Anita was not the meek, obedient sort. She would say what she felt without holding back. She could go to great lengths for her ideals. In this regard she may even have been more fierce than Chitra. And let's face it: there's a vast difference between the moral underpinnings of a business family and the household of a salaried teacher. I feared right then that her presence in our home would be the cause of much turmoil.

The biggest disappointment for Anita after we returned home was the matter of my employment. She'd asked me in Ooty: "How much leave do you have?" The moment is as vivid to me as if it were happening in front of me right now.

We were returning to our room after breakfast and she asked the question just as my hand was reaching out to unlock the door. We had woken up late that day and rushed down to make it to the hotel's breakfast. She had told me as we were eating, "This waking up late is unheard of in my house. Everyone is done with breakfast by eight. And Appa's lunch box is ready, too." Having begun, she took me through the rest of the daily routine in their house. Her father, she explained, had a very sensitive stomach, which he protected by never eating or drinking anything outside home other than the occasional coffee. This meant that his lunch had to be ready before he left for the university. Her mother, she recounted with some pride, would be up before dawn so that breakfast for everyone and a lunch box for her father could be ready before eight. "Appa would leave for university before we left for school," she said and laughed. "He'd spend an hour or so in the library before going to his department. When his classes for the day were done, he'd spend some more time in the library, then return home by seven in the evening."

After speaking about her family's routine through most of breakfast, she went quiet as we returned to the room. Perhaps she was thinking of how her day would change after we returned home, how it would have to reshape itself to accommodate my workday. Then, as I unlocked the door, she asked me how much leave I had taken from work.

We entered the room. I closed the door and encircled her waist with my arm.

"I'd take permanent leave to be with you," I said, trying to brush the question off.

"No, I'm serious. I really want to know. Tell me how much leave you have," she said.

"I just told you," I said. "It's the truth. I'm on endless leave now that you're here."

She asked again, but I managed to make light of the matter and leave it at that.

I don't know all that Sripati had said while the marriage talks were on, but I believe she was told I was the director of Sona Masala. Which was, of course, true. The fact that I didn't have anything to do with the running of the business is another matter altogether.

We returned from Ooty on a Saturday afternoon. The rest of the day was spent recovering from the bus journey and unpacking our bags. We had shopped with such abandon in the Ooty market that we couldn't even remember all that we had bought. One by one, the objects emerged from our bags to surprise us. Handcrafted trinkets, a coffee mug, an assortment of hair clips, a packet containing the seeds of some flowering plant, a picture frame—all sorts of things. Anita had bought a serving spoon with a carved handle for Amma, a stand on which to rest his spectacles for Appa, an ornamental box of dried fruit and three kinds of chocolate for Malati, and a small water jug for Chikkappa.

The practice of giving gifts to people who live in the same house was new to us. In the pre–Sona Masala days, before we moved to the new house, all purchases were discussed among the whole family. Whether it was clothes for Malati, a sari for Amma, trousers for me, or new spectacles for Appa, everyone knew what was being bought. Nothing new entered the house as a surprise. We even planned and plotted what new clothes were to be bought for Deepavali. We'd list our requirements and buy what was possible with the money available. The rest could wait until the next opportunity arose to shop. How were any of us to know the sense of anticipation associated with opening a gift-wrapped package? Even if we could have afforded it, there's something absurd about exchanging gifts when it's all paid for from a single pocket.

It became an occasion of sorts when Appa would tell us how much we could spend. A few weeks before the festival, when all of us were present, Appa might say to me, "Look here, didn't you say you needed trousers? Let's buy you a pair for Deepavali. See what you can get for three hundred . . ." Or, he would say something to the same effect to Malati. That meant a decision had been reached and three hundred rupees each had been sanctioned for me, Malati, and Amma. He had no objection if I bought a shirt and a pair of pants or three shirts as long as it was within the budget. We'd go to make the purchases sometime in the following week or two. If Malati or I bought something that slightly overshot our allotted budget, Amma would make up for it from her share. After he started working, Chikkappa always bought his own clothes and essentials. But my hunch is that he still kept Appa informed. Back then, none of us had the courage to buy anything without involving the others.

Anita had made sure that everything we had bought for the family was gift-wrapped. She kept the presents together on one side of the room as she emptied our bags. Clothes to be washed began to pile up in the corner. She checked the pockets of my trousers and shirts before adding them to the heap, and every time she found coins in my pocket she pretended to be angry at my carelessness. My pockets contained all sorts of scraps of paper—bus tickets, hotel bills, receipts for the things we'd bought, business cards pressed into my hand by shop owners. "You can throw it all away," I told her. "It's rubbish." But those scraps of paper were connected to the time we had spent together in Ooty. She unfolded each one and examined it. She smoothed and stacked some of them on the table. The rest she threw away. We both bathed and waited with some eagerness for dinnertime to arrive. She with genuine excitement, and I hoping that the farce about the gifts would be done with as quickly as possible.

When the call for dinner came, we started to shuffle downstairs carrying the packages. "We must give these out right now, when everyone is together. You hand them over," Anita said.

I didn't know how to get through the situation, but what choice did I have? "No, no. You give it to them," I mumbled.

She arranged it so that I was carrying the ones meant for Appa and Chikkappa. She took the other two. The rest of the family had already gathered by the time we reached the dining table.

"Anita has bought some things for you all in Ooty," I announced cheerfully to Amma, but loud enough for everyone to hear. My words sounded hollow even to me. My only aim was to put an end to this as soon as possible. I briskly handed Appa his package. I placed Chikkappa's in front of him and said, "This is for you." Meanwhile, Anita had given Amma and Malati their presents.

Anita was as enthusiastic as I was awkward. She took Appa's gift, said, "Do you know what this is?," and unwrapped it herself to produce the stand. "You can keep your glasses on this when you sleep or go for your bath. That way, the lenses will not get scratches on them." Appa took off his spectacles twice and put them on the stand with the air of someone rehearsing. Meanwhile Chikkappa had unwrapped his water jug and placed it on the table.

"You can keep this in your office," Amma suggested.

"Yes," he said. "Good idea. I'll take it in with me to-morrow." He walked over to the small table where he kept his keys and made room for the jug. He believed that if you didn't want to leave home without something, you kept it near your keys.

Malati looked at her dried fruits and chocolates and joked, in the voice of a child, "This is all for me. I'm not going to share it with anyone." She placed them on the steps leading upstairs.

Amma looked at her carved serving spoon, said, "We can use this when there are guests," and went into the kitchen to leave it there.

I was happy that it had all gone quickly and unevent-fully, but it seemed to me there was a strain in the air. I could sense that there was something left unsaid. One of them must have been struggling not to point out that it's all very well to blow money when it isn't yours. Had the money I spent been unquestionably mine, I would have had no hesitation in joining the festivities. I could have been as giddy as Anita. But in this house there were such intricacies to the flow of money that it meant something entirely different for me to spend my money than for Anita to spend it. In any regular household, family members glare when a wife begins to freely spend her husband's hard-earned money. What to say of our house, then, where it was all far more peculiar and convoluted?

When I was in high school, Amma would say that she expected a sari from my first paycheck. "May the job be such that it's a silk sari," she'd say, half joking. There was a dramatic quality to that gesture that made it enter my daydreams: buying Amma a grand sari with my first earnings became part of the shining future I imagined for myself. It was one of the things that kept me going through the strain of preparing for exams. Then Sona Masala became successful, and somewhere along the way that sari evaporated from Amma's words and my dreams. No one realized when I began to earn money. I didn't even realize it myself. When I started working at Sona Masala, a bank account was opened in my name and I received a set of business cards. Some months later, I looked at the passbook and saw that an identical amount was accruing in my account every month. That's when it struck me that I was getting a salary. It would have been meaningless, of course, to go through with the ritual of buying Amma a sari then.

That evening, as I ate, I began to fear that those unsaid

words among us would soon fester and spread their stench. I gobbled up what was on my plate.

Amma noticed and tried to keep me there longer. She said, "Don't be in such a hurry. I'm going to serve some fruit after everyone's finished. We have some excellent apples."

"I've had enough. I'm exhausted from the journey and can barely eat what you've already served me. Sleep is all I want now," I told her, and with that I fled.

The next day was a Sunday. We lazed about in the morning, took a nap in the afternoon. And then, as we sat drinking tea, Anita again brought up the matter of my going to work. With the wedding and honeymoon done with, she must have assumed I'd be going back to work on Monday. I was sitting on the bed in our room, sipping from a teacup. She was in a chair opposite me.

"Are you unhappy you have to go to work tomorrow?" she asked, trying to mollify me.

I drank the last of my tea in a gulp and placed the cup on the table: "I'm not going anywhere," I said. "The job can go to hell."

She thought I was joking, an indulgent husband telling his new wife that his work was insignificant compared to her. She looked pleased. "Shall I pack you a lunch box for tomorrow?" she asked.

"Ayyo, there's no need. Let it be," I said. "I've never

been fussy about food. You shouldn't worry about it, either. In any case, my work hours are quite flexible." I didn't want the conversation to proceed any further. I left the room.

From the next day on, Anita began to acquaint herself with our domestic routine. Chikkappa got ready and left at half past eight in the morning. If breakfast wasn't ready in time, he would leave without eating, but he would never be late. By the time he left his phone had already started ringing with urgent matters. You only had to see him in the morning—rushing about, coming down the stairs even as he buttoned his shirt, distractedly gulping down whatever breakfast was placed in front of him, grabbing his keys with a flourish—to know that here was a man deeply involved with his work. If he answered a call, everyone went absolutely quiet. The household's rhythm slackened once Chikkappa left for work. Nothing else that happened in the house was really time-bound.

Anita witnessed this flurry of activity on Monday morning and grew worried that I was going to be late. She came up and woke me.

"Don't rush me. There's still time for me to leave," I said, in a listless tone. I soon got up as usual, without any hurry. Then I had tea while glancing through the paper, took a bath, and came down for breakfast.

Amma announced, "He likes *dosas* only when they are

hot," and proceeded to pour them out one by one as I ate. In the interval between *dosas* I looked at Anita and winked. My lack of urgency must have confused her as she tried to understand how best to help me prepare for my day. Finally, she folded a handkerchief and gave it to me before I stepped out. It was ten o'clock when I left.

I was back by half past three. If Anita was surprised she didn't bring it up. The next day I returned at one, had lunch, and slept through the afternoon. The day after I didn't step out all day and stayed in bed on the pretext of a headache.

On the fourth day, I had finished my bath, put on my clothes, and was combing my hair in front of the mirror when Anita entered the room and closed the door behind her. She sat on the bed and in a firm voice began to ask me some difficult questions. By then she must have perceived Chikkappa's status in the house and guessed what was going on.

"Tell me the truth," she said. "What exactly is your work? Whose income does this house run on? Why don't you ever speak about your job? Where is it that you go every day?"

She said she would not eat until I told her. I crumbled. I thought that at least my wife should know the truth. So I let her have the entire story of our household and everyone in it.

I told her, "There's no dearth of anything. It doesn't matter who's doing what as long as it all runs smoothly. There's lots of money in the family. Don't worry about it."

Her reaction was not what I expected.

"Why did you cheat me?" she asked, furious. "Why did you marry when you are living off others? I don't need all this. I can survive on very little. But I want you to have a respectable job, whatever it is. Can you not at least go to the warehouse regularly and accept only the pay you deserve for your work? How can you not feel ashamed of living off alms?"

I tried to calm her down. At one point I brought up Appa's share in Sona Masala and said, "Look, it's all ultimately ours, isn't it?" This disgusted her. It was an inheritance, she said, and there was no telling what could go wrong. Above all she simply could not accept the fact that I had no personal income. In my thinking, what came to the family was mine. In her mind, my family and I were separate entities.

She sat on the bed and wept for a long time. In between sobs she said things like: "If it comes to that I can start working, too . . . Everyone should want to stand on their own feet . . . You can't just live off others . . ." There was no pacifying her.

To tell the truth, her words had found their mark deep inside me. My situation was something I often thought about. But how was I to extricate myself from it? There was little chance I would find a good job now. I had no real skills to speak of. I told her: "Look, I've been going to the warehouse all along. It's only been irregular since our wedding. I'll start again from tomorrow and be sure to work hard." There was no other way to console her.

She soon calmed down. She washed her face so no one could tell she had been weeping. I sat there silently looking at her. "Why don't you start right now," she said, and left the room.

All this went on in the privacy of our room, behind a closed door. But Amma is alert to these matters and she probably guessed that something like this had transpired.

That night I noticed something that spoiled my sleep. I remembered seeing the receipts for the things we bought in Ooty stacked on my table until that very morning. Just before I turned in, I noticed they were gone. I looked around and found them in the dustbin—crumpled. It could only have been Anita. But I didn't ask her about it.

I tossed and turned in bed for a long time. Scenes of Anita and me shopping in Ooty kept coming to mind. I would experience sudden gushes of affection for her and feel like buying her something or other. It was an inexplicable feeling, this wanting her to want something, then meeting that want, and that somehow drawing us closer. As we walked through the market in Ooty, I'd follow her into every stall she entered and encourage her to buy something. The first time we returned from the market she asked shyly, "Did I spend too much?" I told her, "If that happens I'll let you know. Don't worry about money." Not that we were spending any great amount on the trifles we bought. Even so, whenever possible she'd try to bargain and bring the prices down. Somehow, I found this regard she showed for my money gratifying. And it gave me great pleasure when she asserted her right over my money and asked me to pay the shopkeepers: "Give him thirty-five"; "Two hundred here"; "Twenty-five." All the days we were in Ooty, we never returned from the market empty-handed. It must have been hard for her to throw away those receipts, with all those memories attached to them. I certainly know it was difficult to see them lying crumpled in the dustbin.

I started going to work regularly at the Sona Masala warehouse. I would leave at nine in the morning and return only after dusk. I intended to work hard, but my resolve didn't last long. The same old reason—there wasn't any work for me to do. But my bank account began to see a larger deposit every month. Chikkappa must have felt I needed more now that I was married. The sum was significantly larger than what we needed for our expenses, but Anita's needs had little to do with money.

A man in our society is supposed to fulfill his wife's financial needs, true, but who knew he was expected to earn the money through his own toil? As I came to terms with Anita's ideas of self-reliance, my attendance record at the warehouse could match that of the most assiduous of employees. Only Chikkappa knew how little work I actually did. I had mentioned Coffee House—where my attendance was equally impressive—to Anita. She must have thought it was a small eating joint near the warehouse. I never took her there, of course, but I mentioned the oracular Vincent to her in a lighthearted way.

Anita was never shy of speaking her mind, especially when she disagreed with something that was happening around her. That was the nature of her upbringing. The unwritten rules of our house were the very opposite. We went on as if nothing had happened. For instance, no one objected to anything Chikkappa did or said, especially after we moved to the new house. No one asked questions when he boasted that government officials were friends of the Sona Masala company. The only notes of discord were Appa's occasional reminiscences of his days working as an honest salesman for an upright company. When he would say such things, we pretended not to hear, and Amma would try to steer the conversation elsewhere. We put Appa's behavior down to his chronically gloomy outlook, but I suppose we knew deep down that he was right. After all, we used to help him with his work, and the difference between then and now was stark. Sona Masala might have been our firm, but none of us knew anything about the business. In the early days of Sona Masala, Appa would go to the warehouse. But he soon realized his outlook was very different from Chikkappa's, and that his presence there could only cause trouble. He withdrew and left the running of the business to Chikkappa.

We wouldn't dream of challenging Appa or Chikkappa, no matter what. True, there was some self-interest involved, but it would be an exaggeration to say it was only that. It was a difference of culture, too. Sometimes, Anita would fly into a rage after sparring with Malati and Amma and resort to snide remarks about Appa or Chikkappa. The rest of us would fuss about lest they heard her. Amma valued the household's well-being more than winning the day's fight. She would surrender at once, and Anita would feel she had emerged the victor. So when the family was together there was always a slight air of dread regarding what verbal bomb Anita might drop next.

The house next to ours was lying vacant, so we rented it to stock spices where we could keep an eye on them. Lorries with sacks of spices would arrive on some nights at about nine and leave empty after an hour. Once, a lorry arrived late, at around eleven. The sound of the engine woke me. Anita, her sleep disturbed, began to grumble. I didn't like it. Perhaps she hadn't yet comprehended that this trade was our source of sustenance. I got up and, without turning on the light, went and stood at the window. Our room was on the second floor, overlooking the street. Chikkappa was already outside. The lorry had brought two workmen. The driver asked them to unload the lorry quickly so they could leave, but Chikkappa protested. He insisted that each sack be weighed as it was unloaded. The unloading went on, slow and systematic. Anita joined me at the window. She must have wondered why I wasn't helping Chikkappa, but she said nothing. There was an argument on the street below: Chikkappa protesting about the weight of some sacks; the driver claiming our weighing scale was faulty. While this was happening, one of the workmen injured his foot—it caught the side of the metal gate while he was bringing in a sack. Chikkappa rushed into the house, emerged with some old cloth, and bound his foot. Chikkappa then climbed into the lorry and began hauling sacks out of the truck and onto the back of the other workman. There was a practiced ease to his movements that only a workman could have. I returned to the bed and lay down on my back. I couldn't fall asleep.

The silence of the night had yielded to the curt talk

among workers, the sound of their labored breathing. Finally the chains at the back of the lorry clattered, the engine came to life, and the lorry left at around one. Anita stood there until then. I didn't ask her why. She went to bed afterward without speaking.

SEVEN

The day Amma chased away that woman, Chikkappa didn't emerge from his room until he was called for lunch. We all sat at the table, with the exception of Amma, who usually ate after the rest of us had finished. She served us *chapattis*. Conversation was terse, restricted to "Can I have some of that?," "That's enough," and the like. Amma tried to get us to talk as we usually did, asking, "How has the curry turned out? I didn't have any dill or it would have tasted better."

No one answered.

After a moment Anita said, "Oh, but *masoor dal* curry goes very well with *chapatti*. If you had been more careful this morning we could all have had some."

The very thing we'd been trying to skirt, the specter Amma had been trying to dispel, was dragged to the table by Anita. There was a silence during which everyone concentrated intensely on their plates. I wondered who would come to Chikkappa's aid. As in the morning, it was Amma who stepped forward.

"Do you know what you are saying?" she asked, her voice low and menacing.

Anita seemed undaunted, even gleeful. It only remained to be seen if this battle would continue to be fought through insinuation or if she would step into the ring and have it out.

"What do you mean? Maybe there's no one else here who likes *masoor*, but I do. I wish you had taken it," she said.

Amma raised her voice: "If beggars from the street come to our house should we welcome them?"

The rest of us were quiet. I felt I should say something to Anita to silence her, but I couldn't think what.

Anita went on: "How many beggars from the street have been known to bring us food?"

Amma said, "What is that woman to you? Why are you speaking on her behalf? Does she matter to you more than your own family?"

"She's nothing to me. She may be something to someone here, but not to me. I just don't like how we chased her off like a stray dog without even listening to her. If women don't support other women, who will?"

"So to support women you'll indulge just about any home wrecker?"

"What makes you think she's a home wrecker? She hasn't cheated us or asked anything of us. It's possible she has been betrayed, but certainly not the other way round."

Chikkappa raised his glass of water and gulped it down. He pushed back his chair and left the room with food still on his plate. I supposed something was expected of me then. "Stop it now, Anita," I said. She carried on eating as if nothing had happened.

"You've snatched his meal from him," Amma said, shaking with fury.

"You're talking about yourself," Anita said. "You spilled the curry that was meant for him."

Amma then brought out her most powerful weapon, one she had used many times to silence us. "Am I doing all this for myself?" she asked.

Anita was unmoved. "Yes, you are doing this for yourself," she said. "You want to ensure that Chikkappa remains unmarried. You can't stand the thought of anyone else entering this house and challenging your authority."

Amma reeled from Anita's words. Appa had raced through

his meal without saying a word, and now he, too, got up and left. Malati had been quiet until now, but seeing Amma defeated and close to tears, she stepped in.

"We're not in the habit of entertaining riffraff. Today it's her, tomorrow someone else. Then old classmates. If we start laying out chairs for people we'll soon be on the street with a begging bowl. Who doesn't want to be connected to the wealthy? There'll be hundreds of people who will cook up stories with an eye to making quick money."

Anita let her reference to her old classmate go. She said, "There's no smoke without fire. If he lacks the courage to stand by her, he shouldn't have gone near her in the first place."

So far we'd managed to keep Chikkappa happy, with nothing unpleasant ever falling on his ears. The well-being of any household rests on selective acts of blindness and deafness. Anita had outdone herself when it came to suicidal forthrightness. It looked like she wanted to destroy all of us along with herself.

Amma and Malati glared at me with helpless fury. I expect they were unhappy with my silence. Malati said, "Finish your lunch and leave with your tail between your legs." What was I to do? I knew as well as they did that no good would come of Anita's brashness. She needn't have taken that woman's side with such enthusiasm. But I could not dispute what she was saying, either. In any case, Anita seemed satisfied with what she had done. She ate without hurry and went to our room.

A line had been crossed that afternoon. I wondered with some dread about what would come of it. The others in the family must have, too. Anita was to leave that evening for a week in Hyderabad. I just hoped she would manage to leave the house without any further calamity. I went up to our room and tried to avoid talking to her by pretending to fall asleep at once. Anita must have realized I was faking. She kept muttering as she packed: "You could have opened your mouth and said what happened was wrong . . . It's not even as if you have to oblige them anymore . . . You're working as hard as anyone else . . . Just because a woman is unknown doesn't mean she deserves contempt . . . Would you have kept quiet if that happened to a woman from your family? The only decent person in this house is your father but the rest of you behave like he's insane . . . One day I should go to the police and tell them everything I know about this family's affairs . . . Let the dirt come out into the open. Maybe I should go this very day on my way to the train station . . ."

Those last words of hers sent a chill through me. The word "police" had always filled us with a strange fear. Even when all was well, we tended to be on edge in the presence of the police. But there are those who revel in that sort of thing. Chitra was one of them. She spoke of visiting the police station as others mention going to the post office. It was the same with Anita—the result I suppose of her having volunteered for an NGO in Hyderabad. I thought it best not to say anything and kept my eyes closed.

I didn't know how to make her see the relationships in our family from the inside. There was no other way to comprehend them.

I saw her off at the train station. There was only perfunctory talk between us. "All right, see you," she said when she took her seat in the train compartment, the words sounding like a formality. Neither of us seemed keen on speaking to the other. I remained standing in the compartment for a couple of minutes. Then I thought there wasn't any reason to stay, so I left and stood aimlessly on the platform. When I next peeped in through the window, I saw she had already started a conversation with the woman sitting beside her. Anita was wearing a cream-colored sari, her hair gathered in a bun. I wondered at how beautiful she looked in the evening light.

We could easily send her home by plane, but she insisted on going by train. Second class, at that. At least she had agreed to travel in a sleeper compartment.

As the train's departure time neared, the bustle on the

platform grew more frenzied. I didn't know if Anita had seen me standing outside. I tried to attract her attention from the window. She seemed to glance in my direction but perhaps not, because she immediately resumed the conversation with her neighbor. The engine sounded its horn. A couple that had arrived at the last minute was scrambling to get into Anita's compartment with far too many bags. I watched them, fascinated, and during that time the train began to move. I realized I hadn't waved goodbye to Anita and began to walk with the train. She was still engrossed in talking with her neighbor and didn't look toward the window. I ran a few steps as the train gathered speed. Whether she saw me or not, I waved, at least to comfort myself, and then stopped running. The train went on, leaving me behind. I realized I didn't know when exactly we had lost contact. Was it when she began talking to the woman next to her? Or was it when I became engrossed in watching the couple struggling to board? Or was it sometime before that? It didn't feel like I had really seen her off. A feeling came over me of not having done what I'd set out to do.

When I got home, Chikkappa had gone somewhere. Appa was out, too. No trace of Malati. I was in no mood to talk with Amma, who was watching TV. I rushed upstairs to my room and closed the door.

I sat on the bed and the first thing I noticed was that the

door of Anita's wardrobe was slightly ajar. I got up to close it completely, but it didn't move. Some garment was stuck in the crack of the door. I opened the two doors of the wardrobe wide so I could get rid of the obstruction. A familiar smell washed over me. I lost myself for a second in my own reflection in the mirror on the inside of one of the doors. The tall compartment to the right had her saris, arrayed on hangers. On the shelf below were folded tops, *salwar-kameezes*. The locker on the left contained her necklaces, earrings, bangles. Nothing too expensive—it was all mixed metal. With the exception of her *taali* she never wore gold jewelry.

I pulled open one of the two drawers. It had some of her certificates and other official-looking papers. The other drawer had our wedding album. I flipped through a few of the photographs and put the album back. Next to it were some papers. Some receipts. A scrap with someone's telephone number. I saw a folded newspaper clipping and opened it. It was a death notice for someone named Varaseetalakshmi Shankar. The photo showed a scrawny middle-aged woman with large eyes. She had died the previous June. There was no information about how she had died. Strange, I didn't remember Anita having mentioned her to me. Must be a relative. My mind was running away in all directions and I composed myself.

I had broken into her world when she wasn't around.

She would certainly not have approved in her present frame of mind. Still, I persisted. I sifted through her jewelry, wrapped a string of beads around my fingers. I touched her clothes. I rummaged through her papers. I weighed in my palm a pendant cast in the form of the sun. Anita's entire world was contained in that wardrobe. We had not bought anything together after our time in Ooty. I leaned into one of the shelves, amid the clothes, and breathed deep. It was a smell I could not identify, but I had come to know it so well. I took a sari and sniffed it. The scent seemed to diminish rather than intensify. It was the same with any garment I picked out of the wardrobe. Whatever fragrance the whole wardrobe had was missing in the individual clothes it held. The more keenly I sought it, the further it receded. A strange mixture of feelings I could not quite grasp—love, fear, entitlement, desire, frustration—flooded through me until it seemed like I would break.

The next Sunday, that is, the day before yesterday, we were all together at home. Anita was still in Hyderabad, due to return soon. It was a dull, overcast day. I took a nap after lunch, then lazed about in bed for a while. I got up, washed my face, and, as I came down the stairs for some tea, I saw Amma.

She was sitting alone in the living room staring at the wall. The TV was off. She seemed deep in contemplation. I thought of that night, years ago, when I woke up to find her squatting in the kitchen, gazing at the wall by the glow of a flashlight. "What is it, Amma?" I asked. She started. I had used the same words that night, too, and she'd reacted the same way.

"Come," she said. "I'll make some tea. Didn't feel like making some just for myself so I was waiting for one of you." I could guess what she had been thinking—the chaos Anita had created the previous week, how to clear the muck that had risen to the surface when Anita had stirred up the waters.

I followed her to the kitchen door. The counter was sparkling—Amma always cleaned up after lunch. I stood in the doorway as she made tea. I couldn't help remembering the day we first got our gas stove and how she had made tea with such eagerness. It seemed like only yesterday. Now, as she put water on the stove, she said, "Call Appa. I can make his tea along with ours." I didn't feel like leaving the kitchen. I called out for him, but it was Chikkappa and Malati who came down the stairs. "Good job," Amma said. "Now I can make tea for everyone in one go." She added more water to the kettle on the stove. The clouds thickened outside; the house turned a shade darker. It had been years since she'd made tea like this for the whole family. The last time she had, it was not a happy occasion—it was the day Malati stormed her husband's house and returned with her gold. I had entered the house to find everyone else gathered in the living room, and Amma had gotten up to make tea.

I took out cups and saucers and set them on the table.

That morning Appa had brought home my favorite rusk. It came from a bakery near our old house. He'd been over on that side of town after a long time. I used to find this particular rusk so irresistible that if left to myself I'd eat the whole packet. "It's a good thing he remembered," Amma said. She must have asked him to buy it. It had been a while since Appa had bought anything on his own initiative.

I took one and raised it to my mouth. After all this time it still tasted the same. If anything, it was richer now for evoking a simpler time. I felt light.

We sat down at the dining table, one by one. Only Appa was still missing. Amma was clearly overjoyed at seeing all of us gathered like this. She said nothing, but you could see it in the briskness of her stride, her movements, the way she looked at us. The light from the clouded-over sky dimmed further. Now it felt exactly like our old house. Amma brought out the tea. Malati sang out, "Pour it fast, Amma," as she used to when she was a child. The light, the taste of rusk, all of us close together took us back to the old days. But there was still no trace of Appa.

"Where is our Coffee King?" Chikkappa asked.

That single question eased knots that had tightened over the years. At one time, Chikkappa had given nicknames to everyone in the family, and Appa's had been Coffee King. Chikkappa might say, "Looks like Coffee King has had a long day," or: "Today's sales must have been good. Look at Coffee King's swagger," and you'd see Appa soften.

There was a story behind each of our nicknames. Appa's was given to him on one of our Sunday outings for snacks. We had passed a shop selling coffee powder and noticed a board outside that read, *Coffee King—the king of kings*. Later, Appa and Amma shared a coffee as usual. As Appa slurped his coffee, Chikkappa said, "Coffee King is drinking coffee," and we all laughed.

I had acquired a reputation for grumbling as a boy and so was called Kurkure. Malati was Queen M. "Hello, Queen M, you're looking stunning today," he might say, and her face would light up with pleasure. I've always wondered if she'd have turned out as spoiled without his pampering. Amma was Annadaate, because it was she who fed us all. At times when she kept us waiting for meals, we might call out: "O Annadaate, please Annadaate, won't you give us some food?"

Chikkappa was Jugnu to me and Malati from the time he animatedly described to us a scene from the film *Jugnu* in which Dharmendra descends headfirst down a rope from a high roof to steal a diamond.

These names had more or less fallen out of use once we moved to the new house. We no longer spent enough time in one another's company to invoke them. Even when we did meet, at mealtimes and so on, we tended to be distracted. Had things gone on as before perhaps Chikkappa would have given a nickname to Anita, too.

Amma shouted out to Malati from the kitchen to go call Appa. Malati rushed off and returned with him. He could not have failed to notice the festive air. Amma served us all tea, asked if anyone needed more sugar, then sat down at the table.

"Nothing like the rusk from Appanna's bakery," Chikkappa said.

"Yes. He doesn't skimp on the butter," Amma said.

"He adds milk powder to the dough. He once told me himself," Malati said. "But his rusk costs five rupees more than others."

Appa quoted the saying: "Cakes as good as the coins they cost." It was literally true in this case and we all laughed. Appa beamed. It seemed like years since any of us had acknowledged his jokes.

Chikkappa drank his tea quickly and said to Malati, "Queen M—what do you say to another round of tea?"

"Anything for Jugnu," she said playfully, and got up to go to the kitchen.

"I have something for you," Chikkappa told Malati. When she asked what it was, he said, "First the tea. I'll give it to you if the tea is good."

"At least tell me what it is," she said.

Chikkappa yielded. "Earrings," he said. "I accompanied a friend yesterday while he shopped for his sister's wedding. They were all buying earrings. Thought I'd buy a pair, too."

"Thank you, Jugnu," Malati said. "No one in this house has bought me a thing since my wedding."

I said, "But you're always shopping for yourself."

"Oh, you keep quiet," she said, smiling, and went into the kitchen.

Amma called after her, "The tea powder is on the opposite shelf."

Malati emerged in a few minutes with a large cup of tea. "Hotter and stronger than Amma's," she said, placing it in front of Chikkappa.

He laughed. "As if I wouldn't give them to you regardless," he said. "I bought them for you, after all."

The house had come alive with banter. It was as if Anita's

absence had allowed us to be ourselves again, without inhibi-
tions. Amma was smiling in a way I hadn't seen for a long
time. Appa was in good spirits, too. He launched into some
news from his morning's expedition. "You remember Manjunath who lived on our old street? It seems his father died in
his sleep the other day while he was visiting Manjunath. The
same man who won the best-teacher award . . . They've run
his photo in the paper today."

Malati said, "Wasn't he the one who found it hard to
live in Bangalore and so moved back to his village?"

"Yes, that's him. I stopped by this morning to talk to
Manjunath."

"I don't know," Amma said. "I get the shivers when I
think of that house. Who knows if he died in his sleep or if
it was something else . . ."

"Why do you say that, Amma?" Malati asked.

Appa cut in: "Oh, she's always been suspicious of anything to do with them . . . She said similar things when Manjunath's wife died."

"Of course I did," Amma said. "The whole town knows
Manjunath killed his wife. Wasn't it just after that that the old
man ran off to the village?" She looked at Appa: "Of course,
you would take her side anyway. I wonder what it was about
her . . . All these men would hang around Manjunath's house
on the pretext of wanting to talk to him just to get a glimpse

of her. They'd sit at his shop in groups. She was fine in the evening. How did she end up dead later that night?"

"Amma, whatever you do don't bring these matters up when others are present," Malati said.

"Why should I bring anything up?" Amma said. "Anyway, there is no one else here at the moment. And none of those types who will point out the mustard seed under your feet, but are blind to the pumpkin beneath them."

It was clear whom she was referring to. Everyone laughed; I joined in, too, and regretted it even as I did. I had betrayed Anita.

Chikkappa spoke: "None of you know the whole story about Manjunath's wife. Everyone heard the commotion in the morning about her being unconscious. They saw her being carried into a van and rushed off somewhere. But no one knows which hospital they took her to or what they did there. They returned with the body in the evening. I'll tell you—she was already dead when they left the house. They didn't even go to a hospital. They just drove around all day and returned in the evening with the body wrapped in a white cloth. The police were bribed; the body was cremated hastily. Her family was naïve, too—they were even looking forward to Manjunath marrying her sister. He went back on his word soon enough, of course . . ."

"She wasn't blameless," Amma added. "There was a

terrible fight about her behavior in the night. It seems she said something terrible to her husband and he lost his temper and strangled her. He probably didn't think she would die."

"No one knows how exactly she died," Chikkappa continued. "The family went around claiming she had all sorts of ailments, but it was complete nonsense. She was perfectly fine. Who dies suddenly of natural causes at such a young age? You've got to hand it to Manjunath, though. He's managed to get away with it without any consequences . . ."

There was a long silence. Then Malati chimed in with an altogether different story. There'd been a report in the newspaper about a woman who had died two years ago of burns resulting from a gas leak in the kitchen. It had been proven that her husband's family had planned the accident. "They knew she was the first to enter the kitchen in the morning," Malati said. "So they left the gas on at night and closed the kitchen door. She was on fire as soon as she turned on the light switch. The family didn't come to her help for the longest time despite her screams. She said so in her statement before she died, and the husband and in-laws confessed under questioning. But in court they claimed it was all an accident and that the police forced a confession out of them. They were all released . . ."

"These days murder has become commonplace," Chikkappa said. "People go ahead and kill someone, but then they get caught. Remember that techie who recently killed his wife? He was caught because of his overplanning." He laughed.

Malati said, "You're talking about that Suniti murder, right? The poor fellow was caught despite using two SIM cards to hide his location. She was my friend's brother's colleague. Very argumentative at work. And apparently with her in-laws as well. No wonder he was driven to get rid of her."

"The idiot," Chikkappa said. "He confessed that he killed her because she wasn't taking care of his parents. She's dead and he's in jail. Who's taking care of them now? If only he had planned a little better . . ."

Malati asked what he could have done.

Chikkappa sighed. "This is what happens to people who think they know everything just because they are educated and have watched a few films. You should hear Ravi talking about his gang's exploits. Some of the accidents they've planned are simply unbelievable."

"Who? Your friend Ravi?" I thought Malati's voice sounded a touch more excited than it needed to be.

"The very same. You should hear him and his friends making plans—theirs is an entirely different world. He once told me that the murder weapon is crucial in murder cases that go to court. So the best way to protect oneself is to not have a weapon at all."

"Meaning what? Use one's hands?"

"That's what I asked, too. He said to stop being silly. No, they have all sorts of ways. They have people come in from faraway states who vanish as soon as the job is done. Say a man is walking on a lonely street and a vehicle without plates knocks him to the ground and speeds away. Who are you going to catch? Ravi said it's those who kill in anger, smash someone's head in, or stick a knife into their victim . . . They're the ones who get caught. Not the levelheaded ones. Think about it, there are so many ways a person could die . . ."

"What are you people saying?" Appa asked. He looked upset. "You're talking as if it's all right to kill someone when it suits us."

Chikkappa sighed. "Coffee King is living in another age," he said. "These things are not as big a deal today. I haven't brought it up before—but do you know how much I pay as protection money on behalf of Sona Masala? Everyone else does it, too. You never know when you might need these people. It's practically a collective responsibility of businessmen now to ensure they are looked after . . ."

There was an awkward silence. We all knew Appa hated anything even mildly unscrupulous. Usually we made sure no such talk came up—what if he reacted in some extreme way? What if he decided he'd had enough of all this and gave away his money?

As usual I hadn't said anything, but my very silence implicated me. Appa got up and left; then the rest of us, too, one by one.

I rushed to Coffee House in some agitation. As Vincent placed my coffee on the table, I said to him distractedly that I hoped his family was well. He nodded, and with a faint smile said, "Blood is thicker than water, isn't it, sir?"

I began to shiver at the mention of blood. Whatever the meaning of the saying, why should he bring up blood at a time like this? He was at least kind enough to pretend not to notice my discomfort. He went away without speaking another word.

Now it's Tuesday. Anita hasn't called since she left. Going by the ticket I booked for her, she should have been back yesterday afternoon. I haven't returned home since I left yesterday morning. Haven't been able to summon the courage. Slept on the sofa in my office at the warehouse. Roamed here and there all morning, and now I'm at Coffee House. It's imperative I speak to Vincent. I keep telling myself everything is fine but I can't convince myself. Why hasn't she called? She would have if she'd arrived. No one else has called, either. Chikkappa saw me this morning, but said nothing.

I'm sitting here, waiting anxiously. For what, I don't know. The phone rings. I grab it and look at the screen. An unknown number.

I answer: "Hello?"

A voice at the other end: "Hello, Gopi, is that you?"

No, it's not.

"Wrong number," I say, not very politely, and hang up. My mind is in a whirl. Why today of all days must I receive these useless calls? First that insurance agent, now this. Could it be a sign?

Maybe Anita hasn't returned from Hyderabad. Or maybe she's back and hasn't called because she's still mad at me. Could she have had an accident on her way from the train station? What if a lorry slammed into her as she got out of the auto-rickshaw outside our house? Or could something have happened to her after she came home? What if she's killed herself? Everything she might need is there. A roll of rope, electric current, sleeping pills. A tall building not too far away. Two women to goad her—what agent of death is as discreet as words?

Enough of this madness! Let me go home now. I reach for the glass of water in front of me. It shatters in my hand. Vincent comes running, folds up the tablecloth, making sure none of the water falls on me. He seats me at the next table and brings another coffee without my having to ask.

I sit there trying to compose myself, sipping the coffee with some determination.

As he's passing by on his way to another table, Vincent says, "Sir, you may want to wash your hand. There's blood on it."

I freeze. What is happening? What have I become entangled in? There must be some way out of all this. The words rush into my head of their own accord: *ghachar ghochar.*

ACKNOWLEDGMENTS

The author and translator thank: their agents, Shruti Debi and Anna Stein; the editors of the Indian edition, Ajitha G.S. and Shantanu Ray Chaudhuri; for the enormously perceptive comments and edits that shaped this edition, Lindsey Schwoeri; and the others at Penguin USA who helped bring this book to its final form, including Patrick Nolan, Emily Hartley, Roseanne Serra, Colin Webber, and Elke Sigal.